Playinground

by

Susan Hutchins

Playinground

New Edition

British Library Cataloguing-In-Publication Data
A catalogue record of this book is available from the British Library.

ISBN 978 1 9160531 0 6

Published via pgprintandofficeservices.co.uk

Acknowledgements

I would like to thank: Vivienne Evans, Terry Elliot, and Sara Clark for their encouragement and support; Paula Good for her help with copy-editing and proofreading; Chris Dart of DartWorks Design for the cover; and my daughter, Marti Rice, for giving me her blessing when I told her I was going to publish this story.

Introduction

The 1976 heatwave brought gypsy skirts and miniskirts, hot pants, hipsters, cheesecloth and see-through blouses out into the sun.

The contraceptive pill and legal abortion arrived in the sixties; they gave a new-found freedom, made way for free love, open marriage and wife-swapping.

Pattie and Linda are caught up in a sexual revolution; it offers Pattie a solution to her loveless, sexless marriage, gives Linda a means of escape from her controlling, violent husband. Although this is 1976, liberated women still feel it's the men that hold the reins.

Chapter 1

~ July, 1976 ~

Even at this hour of the morning you can feel the heat, can almost see it rising from the tarmac. In the past few weeks the grass that surrounds the playground has become like straw; already the big beech tree is starting to lose its leaves. It's hard to believe August is still a week away.

When the city woke to a bright blue sky five weeks ago, everyone took advantage of the weather; they put on last summer's flares and hot pants, went shopping for the latest in gypsy skirts and see-through blouses. Everyone thought it wouldn't last long, that the heatwave would be interrupted by a cloud or two sooner or later; they expected to change the brightly coloured clothes for a raincoat, or at least a cardigan before the week was out. But flaming June became sweltering July, from sunrise to sunset the sun sent out its rays, blessed the children with tans that made their white cotton socks gleam against their brown legs. It kissed the women's cheeks, brought out the blonde and copper highlights in their hair, and a riot of colour and bronzed flesh into the playground.

Unless you knew the mothers and children that are gathering around the school door, you'd be hard pressed to guess who had vol-au-vents or beef olives for supper, who dined on beans and chips, who lives in a few rooms, who enjoys the luxury of a Georgian house, whose father is a doctor, whose husband a dustman. There are still a few families that are local to the area, families that can remember having to traipse the mile to Royal Hill and then the steep climb to the small Victorian school at the top. They never thought that this once desirable suburb of the city would become fashionable again. They hadn't taken much notice of the garlic and dried spaghetti, the herbs and spices that began to creep into the corner shop. It was after the builders descended on old Joe's pickle shop, when it became home to a smart young couple with a shiny red Mini and a white Lotus parked outside that they began to notice the scaffolding, the restoration being done on the once elegant terraces. Then Woolworths moved from Regent Street and almost overnight the empty building materialised into an antique market; the chippie became an expensive fish restaurant and the council built a posh new school.

It's now 9 o'clock. The door opens. The women kiss the children goodbye and watch them run into school, then they leave the playground. Only Pattie and her eight-year-old son Dylan remain. Dylan is looking anxiously towards the school gate. 'But why isn't he here?' he wails. 'We always go in together. I don't want to go without him.'

'You'll have to,' insists his mother. Her Irish accent raises an octave and she snaps, 'Maybe he's not coming. Maybe he's ill.'

'He was alright yesterday. We're rehearsing this morning. He has to be here. I can't be Tweedle-dum without him being Tweedle-dee!'

'Well, we can't stand out here waiting! You have to go into school.'

Suddenly he pulls his hand from Pattie's and waves. 'Here he is! Ben!' he shouts. 'Hurry!'

Pattie looks towards the gate. Ben is running across the playground towards them. Linda is hurrying behind him, her wrap-around skirt parting with each stride she takes.

'Sorry we're late,' gasps Linda. She bends to kiss Ben's curly head and her long dark hair falls like a curtain; her figure is hardly more than a straight line as she waves the boys goodbye. Pattie is reminded of a Botticelli Madonna, when Linda turns and gives her a tired smile. She wonders, if Linda didn't have to get up at God knows what time to clean the chemist shop, if she put on a bit of make-up, would she be more beautiful or less?

'I thought I was going to get away early,' explains Linda as they walk towards the school gate. 'Then Mr Thomas wanted the glass shelves cleaned. Some of those medicine bottles have been there years so I had to wash them. I don't know what I'd do without Mrs Jones, I don't, honestly. She might be a bit of a fuddy-duddy, but she loves Ben, and he doesn't mind going down and sitting with her, though I think half the attraction is the jar of sweets she keeps.'

'What are you doing now?' asks Pattie as they leave the playground.

'I've just got time to go home and do a bit of housework before going to Mr Roberts.'

'I'm surprised you still do that job. It sounds like you'd need a peg on your nose to go into the building, let alone clean it.'

'Well it's money. I just get on with it. When I take Ben, I put the pornographic magazines out of his reach. What about you? What are you up to?'

'It's too hot to do anything much. I'll prepare a bit of lunch for Andrew; he's working from home this afternoon.'

'That'll be nice.'

'I don't know about nice; he'll be in his office marking papers. Is Brian home?'

'No, he's working.'

'When's he back?'

'Some time after six.'

When they reach the top of Pattie's road, they stop. 'I think I'll make an appointment with the hairdresser,' says Pattie. 'This perm cost over ten pounds. I want them to put it right. I never asked for an Afro! Mind, the sun hasn't helped; it's completely dried it out.'

'I'm taking Ben to the park after school. It's so much cooler than being at home. I'll make a few sandwiches. Would Dylan like to come?'

'That'll be grand. Dylan would love it.'

'I'll drop him back to you about five. Would that be okay?'

Pattie says goodbye then hurries along the tree-lined street. She stops outside a large Victorian semi-detached house and glances up at Andrew's office window. He won't be home till gone twelve, she thinks, which gives her plenty of time to prepare him a cold lunch and get out before he arrives. She opens the gate. Not giving a second look at the wilting standard roses, she walks along the path to the imposing front door. She lets herself in, slips off her sandals, then, enjoying the cool marble tiles beneath her feet, she goes into the lounge. The sun is streaming through the sash windows. Throwing her bag onto the sofa, she has a sudden wish to be back in her parent's house; to stand in their garden and hear the crash of Atlantic waves, feel the wind hitting her face. She would do anything to get away from this heat, would even listen to her mother's persistent complaint about Dylan not being christened; the litany of horror that he'll go to purgatory and won't be buried in consecrated ground. She pulls the shutters together then picks up her bag and leaves the darkened room. Barefoot, she climbs the deeply carpeted stairs. She stops on the landing, stands outside Andrew's bedroom door, then opens it. The room is north-facing and cool compared to the rest of the house. Nothing is out of place; not a sock nor a discarded item of clothing. She gazes at the neatly made bed, trying to remember the last time they had slept together. It would hardly be memorable anyway, she tells herself. She has an overwhelming urge to disrupt the room. She walks towards the bed. Her hands hover over the bedspread. She turns away, worried that the temptation to pull the covers off and throw them across the room is too strong to ignore. She goes to his desk, picks up a pile of papers and flips through them; realising that her irritation is growing, and she might do something she regrets, she puts them down and walks out of the room.

She gazes at herself in the bathroom mirror. The sun has lightened her hair to a strawberry blonde; it has brought a dusting of golden freckles across her cheeks, which makes her look younger than her thirty years. She scowls. All she can see is a mop of frizz. She goes into her bedroom and picks up the phone.

'The perm is a disaster. It looks dreadful. I need something done to it this morning... Yes, that's right, this morning... Yes, a cut and restyle... No, I can't make twelve... Alright; I'll be there at eleven.'

She puts down the phone, goes into her bedroom and takes off her jeans and cheesecloth blouse; she opens her wardrobe and pulls out a cotton maxi dress and a pair of platform sandals. She slips the dress over her head and looks at herself in the full-length mirror. The material's brown and orange sunflower print suits her colouring. The low neckline and tight bodice emphasise her full breasts. She steps into the sandals; the extra height the two-inch platforms give her makes her appear slimmer. She looks good. She smiles, thinking about the afternoon before her. The dress will be removed the minute she climbs into the back of the lorry. There'll be no rush now; she doesn't need to go to the school. Linda's not expecting him home until gone six.

Chapter 2

Thinking about the gossip she'd heard in the playground, Linda makes her way home. The rumour had started when Pattie and her friend Carol had gone to London for a few days to visit an exhibition by an up and coming artist called David Hockney. Linda had immediately dismissed the talk as unfounded. She told the group of gossiping mothers that 'Pattie and Carol are good friends. They both like looking at art. It doesn't mean to say they're lesbians!' She also reminded them that 'only a few weeks ago they were accusing them and their husbands of wife-swapping!'

Linda is wary of getting too involved with the women in the playground; she prefers to keep herself to herself, finds she has enough to contend with in her own life without wasting time listening to a load of trumped-up speculation. Scandal drifts around the playground like a nasty smell, and Linda is certain she's as much a target as anyone else. What she can't understand is why Pattie, who is friendly with everyone, is picked on more than others. She wonders if the root cause is perhaps jealousy. Pattie has everything a wife could want: a lovely home, and a husband who is not only attractive to look at but, as a lecturer at the university, must earn a pretty decent income. And if that wasn't enough, he's happy to let her go away while he looks after their child! Why would she put all that at risk? The newspapers are so full of stories about sex orgies and key parties that people are beginning to think everybody's doing it. Pattie's clothes may be a bit revealing, but that is the fashion. As for wife-swapping, Andrew is far too reserved.

While Pattie was in London, Andrew took and collected Dylan from school. Linda knew Andrew was Pattie's husband - she had seen him with Dylan. But other than a smile and a nod when the boys greeted each other, they had never spoken. When she saw Andrew waiting on his own for Dylan to come out of class she had an urge to say hello. She went over to him. They only said a few words. For some strange reason she had felt constrained, had a sense that Andrew was embarrassed, that maybe he didn't want to be talked to. She understood why; after all, the school playground is a woman's domain; men are a rare sight. When the boys came out of school, she and Andrew went their separate ways. But meeting him left an impression. She'd found his Yorkshire accent fascinating. Had noticed his eyes were the same pale blue as the jacket he was wearing. Had seen the silver streaks in his hair and the way it curled onto his collar. Long hair was fashionable, but she thought the length of his was more out of neglect than style.

The closer Linda gets to home the more she dwells on her own problems. Any love she'd had for Brian is long gone and she is desperate to escape her marriage: a marriage that is not only destroying her and Ben's chance of a peaceful life but is affecting Ben's wellbeing. Now Ben is older he is conscious of what is going on around him. He recognises the change in atmosphere when Brian walks into the flat. Automatically stops the game he is playing and clears the toys from the floor. Accepts without arguing that the television channel is changed to one Brian wants and he must leave the room. She does everything she can to keep the peace. She goes through the motions of being the perfect wife, never complains about a lack of money, or questions where or who he has been with. She makes sure his food is hot and on the table when it is wanted, that his clothes are clean and ironed to his liking. In the bedroom, she is a puppet, a wooden doll that becomes the instrument for his every need.

The thought of 'Leaving Brian' is always with her. She is sure she will be able to manage financially. She will find more work – there are a lot of rich people moving into the area and they are crying out for cleaners. Brian will have to pay maintenance. However, none of those thoughts have helped her find a place to live. She has gone from agent to agent, but no landlord will take on a single mother.

Her one hope is that Brian will leave her for one of the women he tells her about. One of the women he takes into the back of the van when he is working away. But that is wishful thinking; why would he? He has the best of both worlds. It was acknowledged - so he told her - that it is natural for men to have sex with more than one woman. That man has been doing it since time began. Man is the hunter, that's what men do, go out looking for women. He said he didn't believe any bloke who said he only fancied his wife. She knows what he says is rubbish; she only has to think about her own parents' marriage. Her father has been dead five years, but she can remember that loving relationships do exist.

She wonders if her mother suspects something is wrong. Linda had tried to hide the bruises on her arm by wearing a cardigan when she met Gloria in town for lunch, but it had been a sweltering day and Gloria insisted that Linda took the cardigan off. In the end, Gloria grabbed the cardigan and pulled it from Linda's shoulder. Linda told her mother it had been an accident; that she had been going through the door and Brian shut it without realising she was behind him. She doesn't know if Gloria believed her but, of course, it wasn't true; he had slammed the door on her when she had been trying to escape from him. Her mother would be horrified if she knew the whole story. It wasn't only the violence, or the other women. It was far worse than that.

Brian had been talking about wife-swapping for months; he said it would liven up their sex life, that it would satisfy his need for other women. She told him she wasn't interested, but that didn't stop him bringing a couple of swingers back from the pub. She usually did whatever it took to avoid a row, anything not to disturb Ben. This time she let rip; a crying child in the room with them soon had the couple grabbing their coats and leaving.

Linda arrives at a busy road, waits until a gap in the traffic allows her to cross. From there, she walks the few yards to Royal Crescent. She doesn't give the panoramic view across the city a second glance as she treads the uneven stone paving. She stops outside one of the Georgian houses. Like the others, it has seen better days; there are cracks in the rendering, the door desperately needs a coat of paint.

There is always an unpleasant smell in the hallway, a stench of overcooked cabbage and rancid fat from the five flats that occupy the building. The brown lino has been worn down to its hessian backing; the walls have been scuffed by the multitude of people that have brushed against it. If it wasn't for Linda's brightly coloured skirt, you would think the scene had been plucked from a sepia photograph.

She creeps past Mrs Jones's door; when she has a minute to spare, she will call in to see her. She hurries up the curved staircase, reaches the top of the house, notices the bathroom door is open; as it is vacant, she decides to use it. When she comes out of the bathroom, she puts her key in the latch and goes into the attic flat.

Despite the windows being left open, it's like entering an oven. In the winter, the hot colours that decorate the flat give a feeling of warmth, but with the temperature in the 80s the coolest shades of blue will melt. Posters are pinned to the orange walls; fabrics in a mix of purples, reds and yellows hang at the windows, cover the cushions and beds. Linda goes into the sitting room, gathers the Meccano pieces from the floor and puts them into their box. She picks up Ben's books from the seat of the sofa and takes the Meccano set and the books into Ben's room. She goes into the bedroom and opens the dressing table drawer, reaches into the back and pulls out an essay book; she looks at the clock, wondering if she has time to do any writing, decides she hasn't and puts the book back into its hiding place. Brian had complained about the time she spent writing. He doesn't know she is still attending the creative writing course in the local library. She stuffs a pile of dirty clothes into the laundry bag. Taking it with her, she hurries into the kitchen and opens the cupboard door, sorts through the tins of peas, baked beans and spaghetti hoops until she finds a tin of corned beef. She'll use some of it to make sandwiches for the park, buy a few more potatoes to make a hash for Brian. If she's quick and there's no queue in the launderette, she'll have time for a bite to eat before going to Mr Robert's.

Chapter 3

Pattie drives her black Morris out of the city and through the suburbs. Gradually the houses are replaced by fields and she turns off the main road into a narrow back lane. It is the sort of lane frequented by lovers and overnight lorry drivers; today it looks deserted. For a moment, she thinks Brian is not here; then she spots his van partly hidden by shrubs and a canopy of branches. She drives past the van and glances into the empty cab. Then, wondering where he is, she parks the car in front of the van. She turns off the engine, opens the door and steps out onto the dusty ground. Suddenly, Brian appears from behind a hedge of brambles. She watches him as he climbs the step to a stile; with the grace of an athlete, he throws his long legs over it and jumps onto the dirt path. He sees her, gives a wave, then walks towards her. Admiring the tight fit of his jeans, the bulge of muscle beneath his rolled-up shirt sleeves, she stands watching and waiting for him. The denim shirt is open; the sun catches the blond hairs on his chest, turning them to gold. As he gets closer she can see the dusting of hair on his forearm, the mixture of hazel and green in his eyes as he stands in front of her. He smiles, and she rests her palms onto his shoulders, tiptoes her platform sandals to gain height, raises her face to his with parted lips ready to be kissed. He takes his face from hers, holds her away from him, and says, 'Aren't you worried someone might see us?'

'Not here; we're pretty safe,' she murmurs, lifting her face again.

'Come on,' he says, grabbing her hand.

‘Don’t you worry about being seen?’ she asks as they walk towards the van.

‘No. I’ve told you. Linda knows I have other women.’

‘But she doesn’t know about me?’

‘That might be a bit close for comfort,’ he says as he opens the van door. He jumps inside. ‘Quick, get in,’ he tells her. He takes her hand and pulls her up towards him. With his arm around her, he pulls the door and it shuts with a loud clank, blocking out the light. He turns towards her, reaches for the hem of her dress and lifts it over her head. His fingers brush against her breast. ‘Good, no bra,’ he says as he throws the dress aside. His hand feels its way inside her pants. ‘That’s what I like,’ he says. ‘A woman that’s ready and waiting.’

Pattie has had her fair share of lovers, but there’s been no one like Brian. None have matched her enthusiasm for sex the way he has. And it hasn’t waned; it must be all of six months ago when she’d rung Linda’s doorbell to ask her if she would pick Dylan up from school. Brian had answered; he told her Linda was at work and he would pass on the message but was sure it wouldn’t be a problem. Linda was going to the school to get Ben anyway; she’d keep an eye on Dylan until it was time to take him home. However, before Pattie had left the door, they had made a date. Since then, they had met at least once a week.

They are both naked, but heat in the van is stifling; it fills the space like a solid entity. Pattie is oblivious to the soaring temperature; her sex drive has taken her to another plane; the only release from the urge that is consuming her is Brian.

Pattie’s back is pressed against the metal floor. She wraps her legs around him, pulls him towards her. Their sweat makes a seal as he pushes himself into her. They change position; he is now lying beneath her. She sits astride him; the crack around the door brings in a little light. Now her eyes have become accustomed to the dark, she can see his face. He is smiling. Each time she moves he groans with pleasure. Knowing she can satisfy him, that she'll do things that a lot of women with their prissy ways will never do, gives her a sense of power. His shout of pleasure when he reaches his climax causes an orgasm to take her body. Like waves, they travel through her. 'My God,' he says. 'What a girl you are.'

Pattie lifts herself away from him. She reaches for the floor and lies down beside him. She puts her head on his shoulder, rests her hand on his stomach. For a moment, they say nothing. Except for the rise and fall of their breath, they are still. Suddenly, he lifts his hand and ruffles her hair, his voice breaking the peace when he asks, 'What made you get it cut?'

'Linda.'

'Linda?'

'I was talking to her this morning; she's taking Ben to the park after school and offered to take Dylan with her, which means I don't have to dash off. Her hair looked fabulous and she doesn't spend a penny on it. It seems to look after itself. Anyway, I've decided to go natural, no perm, no bleach.'

'God, don't be another Linda. I've enough of Goody-two-shoes at home. I like you the way you are.'

She knows he likes her: why wouldn't he? They are two of a kind. He needs sex as much as she does. It doesn't upset her that other women enjoy an hour or two in the back of the van. What brings on the wave of jealousy is the thought of the school holiday, that Brian will be entertaining his bevy of females while she is stuck at home. She heaves a sigh, 'I'm going to miss you.'

'Why, where are you going?'

He reaches across the floor, takes a packet of cigarettes from his pocket while she tells him, 'School breaks up next week. I'll have Dylan all day. Andrew will be home. We won't be able to see each other.'

He lights the cigarette, takes a long drag before saying, 'I thought Andrew encouraged you to have lovers.'

'He can't give me what I need and accepts I get it from other people; he knows about you, he knows I'm with you this afternoon, but he won't put himself out babysitting Dylan while I'm off having sex with whoever.'

'Well, we'll have to wait until the kids are back at school.'

'Do you remember what we were talking about the last time we met?' she asks.

'Yes. Why do you ask?'

'I've been thinking; wife-swapping could be the answer.'

'I told you, Linda's not interested.'

'If she met someone she was interested in she would be.'

'It's sex I want her to be interested in, not who's doing it to her. I find the thought of someone screwing her exciting; I wouldn't mind watching. But I don't want her having ideas about the bloke. She belongs to me. Anyway, you told me Andrew wasn't happy when you and the Cooks swapped. You said he wasn't able to deliver the goods.'

'Carol was too much of a woman for him. He needs someone understanding, someone soft; someone like your Linda.'

'I don't know how you and Andrew ever got together,' he says as he stubs the cigarette out on the floor. Suddenly, he grabs his jeans and stands up. 'It's like an oven in here,' he says as he pulls them on. He picks up his shirt and puts his hand on the door.

'Hang on. Let me put my clothes on,' says Pattie, reaching for her dress. She pulls it over her head, stands up and slips on her sandals, muttering, 'I don't know why you and Linda are still together. You aren't exactly a match made in heaven.'

Brian opens the door to a flood of sunlight. 'Hurry up. Let's get out of here. I've a wife at home and she suits me perfectly.'

Chapter 4

Mr Roberts is busy unpacking the midday edition of the Evening Post when Linda arrives for work. Eager to get on with her jobs, she gives him a cursory wave and hurries past the counter. He calls her name; she turns to look at him and he leaves what he is doing to walk over to her. 'I'd like you to clean my bedroom,' he says; then, sounding rather embarrassed, he adds, 'I've a friend coming to stay.... a girlfriend. Of course, I'll pay you a bit extra.'

Mr Roberts's bedroom is in the attic. Linda is employed to clean the downstairs rooms of his living quarters and has never ventured to the top of the building, not even to have a peek. It isn't because she respects his privacy; she's as nosy as anybody else. What puts her off is the strong smell of excrement wafting down the stairs. She can only guess that the cause of the stink comes from Mr Roberts's two Alsatians.

The dogs are kept in the shop when she cleans the flat. They seem to be well behaved and always give her a friendly sniff, but she's glad they are kept out of her way - a sink piled high with greasy dishes, a filthy toilet, the revolting feel of cold grey bath water when she pulls dog hair from the plug hole, is enough to contend with. She won't refuse to clean the room. Mr Roberts pays well, and she could do with the extra money. If only it didn't interfere with her plan - the day is baking hot and she wanted to get home and have a bath before collecting the boys from school.

Mr Roberts is waiting for a reply, so she smiles and says, 'Okay, I'll go up now.' She leaves the shop, climbs the stairs to the flat, then, ignoring the smell, she goes up to the attic to assess what needs doing. The landing is dark. Something soft and slippery is beneath her feet. She feels for the light switch. Barefoot and carrying her shoes, she goes back down the stairs and into the shop. She waits for Mr Roberts to finish serving then beckons him over. Not wanting anyone to hear, she shows him the soles of her shoes and whispers. 'It's the dogs; there's mess everywhere. It's all over the carpet; look at them, they're filthy. There's a limit to what I can do.'

She half expected him to tell her he'll find someone else and is unprepared when he says, 'Yes, it's a bit of a mess. I'm sorry.' He puts his hand in his pocket, pulls out a fistful of coins and puts them next to the till. 'Give them to me,' he says as he takes the shoes from her. 'Keep an eye on the shop. There's enough change to keep you going.'

She quite enjoys the few minutes spent behind the counter. She sells a couple of newspapers and is about to add the money for a 'Crunchy Bar' to the loose coins when Mr Roberts calls her name. She turns to look at him; he is standing in the doorway holding her shoes. He beckons her over and she leaves the counter. 'See, spotless,' he tells her as she takes the shoes from him. 'Sorry about that,' he says. 'I know I'm a slob, but as soon as the last customer leaves I'm going to pull up the carpets and get rid of them. Look, do me a favour; give the kitchen and bathroom a bit of a rub then take the rest of the afternoon off.'

Linda arrives home half an hour earlier than usual. What with the long walk as well as the sweltering heat, she is tired. With the aim of having a cool bath foremost in her mind, she puts her key into the latch and goes into the house. Not having the energy to hurry, she takes her time climbing the stairs, is half way up the last flight when she hears the jets blasting from the gas-geyser and a sound of pouring water. She had been hoping that at this hour the Greco family would be at work, but is not surprised; sharing the bathroom with a family of four means you can't rely on it being vacant. Disappointed, she carries on up the stairs and lets herself into the flat. She goes into the bedroom, gathers together her towel and toiletries and carries them to the kitchen. The kitchen and the bathroom share an ineffective party wall that allows the softest sound to be heard, which can be unpleasant, especially during meal times. With her ears alert to any noise that suggests the bathroom is being vacated, she takes the tin of corned beef, a sliced loaf and a slab of margarine from the cupboard. She prepares the sandwiches, fills a bottle with water then puts them into a string bag ready for the picnic. The sound of splashing suggests that the person who is in the bath will be a while, so Linda goes back into the bedroom and removes her essay book from the dressing-table drawer. She sits at the kitchen table, is just about to start this month's writing assignment, when the sound of water gurgling through the pipes makes her jump up. She quickly picks up her towel and toiletries, takes the essay book back to the dressing table drawer, then hurries onto the landing to wait at the bathroom door.

With her hair still damp from her bath and wearing a freshly laundered yellow sundress, Linda taps on Mrs Jones's door. 'My, you do look lovely,' says Mrs Jones when she answers. 'Are you going anywhere nice?'

'Just to school to pick up Ben and his friend; we're having a picnic in the park. I finished work a bit earlier today, so I thought I'd pop in and say hello.'

'That's nice dear, but I'm about to go out myself. My friend Mrs Pugh's invited me for tea. I'd love to chat, but I was supposed to have been there five minutes ago.'

'Well, I won't disturb you. Have a nice time.'

'You too dear; tell Ben I'm looking forward to seeing him in the morning.'

'I will.'

When she leaves the house, Linda has a whole extra ten minutes in front of her. It's a rarity. Usually, she almost has to run the distance to the school. More often than not, she is wearing the clothes she's been working in, has hardly had time enough to put a comb through her hair. Today she is walking at a leisurely pace. A red string-bag swings from her arm. Her hair falls across her shoulders and down the back of the yellow sundress like seaweed on the sand.

At first glance, the playground appears to be almost empty. Then Linda casts her eye around and can see that in every bit of shade, however small, women are sheltering from the sun. Some huddle beneath the beech tree, others try to squeeze a bit of shade from the dying privet, half a dozen or more have retreated into the shadow of the caretaker's wooden shed. Carol Cook and a group of friends have commandeered the dark patch next to the girl's toilet block. Before Linda has time to move out of sight, Carol spots her and beckons her over. Wishing she had arrived at her accustomed last minute, Linda goes to where they have gathered and stands listening to their conversation.

'This heat's killing me.'

'Me too.'

'It's too hot to get near a stove. I rang Edward and told him we're eating out this evening, children and all.'

'We're living on salads.'

'I never thought I'd long to see a cloud.'

'The Government's saying water's only to be used for drinking, washing and toilets.'

'My garden's dead. Not even the weeds can survive.'

'Millions of pounds worth of crops are failing; the price of food's going to go sky high.'

'A wood caught fire in Cornwall.'

'Some parts of the country have stand pipes.'

'Oh God, the last thing I want is to queue with a bucket in my hand.'

'Nobody will be queuing for anything if the reservoirs dry up.'

They shake their heads, heave sighs of despair.

Carol looks towards the school gate, 'Pattie's late.'

'She's not coming,' Linda tells her. 'I'm taking Dylan and Ben to the park.' With that, the school door opens, and a stream of children pour out onto the playground.

The women disperse and move towards the children. Linda spots Ben pushing his way towards her; Dylan is at his side. 'Have you seen Dylan's mum?' asks Ben.

Linda looks at Dylan, 'She had to go out. You're coming to the park with me. Is that okay?... Ben, Dylan! Come back! Wait for me!'

The park is a five-minute walk from the school. It's not exactly a park; there are no swings or slides. What it does offer is a large square of grass, enclosed by a low stone wall. Trees and shrubs make it a good place for hide-and-seek; someone has tied a rope to the branch of an old oak tree. A hundred or so years ago, the four-storey houses that surround the green space would have been home to the wealthy. Now the people who live in them are a mix of white-collar workers and working classes. Those that enjoy the little oasis are mainly mothers and children with no garden of their own. Dylan and Ben make a beeline for the rope. Linda sits under a tree. The grass has almost disappeared; in its place are dry patches of earth, cracks that could swallow a bird.

Linda watches the boys, but her mind is elsewhere. Brian will be home this evening. As always, she wonders what mood he will be in. Thankfully, he will be away again in the morning, but only for one night. He'll be back on Friday and she will have to suffer his tyrannies until he leaves on Monday morning. Weekends! Only she knows how much she hates them. She takes her eyes from the boys, lies with her back on the ground, gazing into the tree branches, picturing the home she hopes to eventually find for her and Ben - a ground floor flat with two bedrooms, a garden where Ben can play. She is thinking about flowers and what she will plant, when she hears Ben say, 'You said we could have ice-cream.'

She sits up. 'Sandwiches first,' she says, pulling the string bag towards her. She hands the boys their sandwiches. In between bites they tell her about the school play.

'Miss Clark said we have to bring food and a drink.'

'It'll be funny having our tea in school.'

'Miss Clark said to tell our mums and dads to come early.'

'They're expecting a lot of people.'

'Is your dad coming?' asks Dylan.

Ben looks at Linda. 'Is he?'

She's not sure how to answer. Brian thinks anything to do with children and school should be left entirely to women. 'You'll have to ask him. Hurry up and finish that sandwich, then we'll buy those ice-creams.'

She hadn't realised how late it was until she notices the clock in the shop. A quarter past five. Brian will be home at six. 'Hurry boys; make up your minds,' she tells them.

They dither between wanting ice-cream and lollies; in the end she asks for two cornets. She watches the shop assistant take two small cubes from the freezer, waits while she takes off the silver paper. Linda looks at the clock again, taps her fingers on the counter as the girl puts the ice-cream into the cornets. Linda pays for them, then ushers the boys out onto the pavement.

She waits at the corner of the road while they catch up with her. 'Come on,' she calls. 'Daddy will wonder where we are.' Licking their ice-creams, they follow her across the road. She chivvies them along as they make their way to Dylan's house.

She had expected Pattie to open the door, is unprepared to see Andrew standing in the doorway. Before either of them has time to speak, Dylan pushes past Andrew, saying, 'Come on Ben, I want to show you my Chopper.' In a flash Ben is through the porch, into the house and out of sight.

'I'm sorry,' says Linda. 'We can't stop. Do you mind getting Ben? We have to go.'

'They'll be in the garden. Dylan's wanted to show Ben his bike since he got it. I was just about to make coffee. Would you like one?'

There is something about Andrew that makes her want to stay. Despite the need to get Ben and go, the words 'Okay, but I can't be long,' escape her mouth.

This is the first time she's been invited into the house. She and Pattie always part company at the corner of the road. She steps inside and follows Andrew into the kitchen. He pulls a chair out from the table, asking, 'How do you like your coffee?'

Linda sits listening to the kettle's whistle, the clatter of crockery and cutlery as she gazes around her. From what she's seen of the house, she's surprised how devoid of colour and paraphernalia it is. Other than Dylan's paintings tacked onto the plain magnolia walls, there is nothing else. Pattie had told Linda she likes to visit art galleries, which is why Linda thought the house would be full of artwork.

Andrew puts two mugs of coffee onto the table then goes to a cupboard. Linda tries to think of something to say, something clever, something that will make him like her. The sound of the boys' laughter coming through the open window causes her to say, 'They sound like they're having a good time.'

Andrew puts a biscuit barrel onto the table then goes to the window. Ignoring the urge to join him, Linda watches him as he stands looking out at the boys. Their eyes meet when he turns away from the window, and he walks towards her saying, 'Ben must come again.' Sitting opposite her, he adds. 'They're in high spirits; what with the holidays, and the play, they don't know how to contain themselves. Is your husband going?'

'To the play? I'm not sure. It depends if he's working.' She chooses not to disclose the fact that Brian would rather be in a pub than at a school play. 'What about you?' she asks.

'Yes, I'll be there.'

There's a lull in the conversation. They both pick up their mugs, sit sipping at their drinks. Feeling the need to break the silence, Linda puts her mug onto the table, saying, 'I wish this weather would change; it's hotter than ever.'

He nods. 'Yes, it's getting everyone down. We're all praying for rain, or at least a cool breeze.'

'Pattie said you might be going to Ireland during the holiday. She told me about her parents' house; it sounds lovely, high on a cliff, overlooking the sea. They'll have plenty of cool breezes there.'

'Pattie might take Dylan... though she says that every year. The last time they went was in seventy-three. What about you, have you got anything planned?'

'No, I'm working. Ben will spend a few weeks with my mother; he loves going there. She spoils him rotten.'

'The sound of a car on the gravel drive distracts him; a flicker of annoyance crosses his face as he stands up. 'Pattie's here. I must get on. I'll see you at the play?'

'Yes, I'll see you there.'

He leaves the room. She notices his drink, hardly touched, has been left on the table. She looks at the clock: ten minutes past six, and walks to the window. Pattie's car is on the drive. She puts her head through the open window. 'Ben, we must go!'

Chapter 5

The first thing Pattie notices when she turns off the engine is that Ben is in the garden. Dylan's bike is lying on the ground; Ben and Dylan are kneeling beside it examining the brakes. They are so engrossed in what they are doing they don't appear to have seen or heard her. Pattie sits with her hands on the steering wheel wondering whether to reverse out of the drive or stay quietly where she is. The last person she wants to see is Linda.

Pattie hadn't expected Linda to be here – Brian is the sort of man that wants his wife putting a meal on the table when he gets in from work. Nor is she prepared for the guilt she feels. After all, adultery is part of the scene these days; it isn't as though she's planning to run off with Brian. Anyway, if what Brian says is true, Linda dislikes sex. When it comes to him wanting what he calls his conjugal rights, she will do nothing more than lie on her back with her legs apart. If Linda knew what she had been doing with her husband this afternoon she might see it as a favour, see it as one less wifely duty she has to perform.

Pattie has got to know Linda quite well. Walking to and from school with her, hearing all about her cleaning jobs, seeing the building she lives in, has made Pattie appreciate things about Andrew that she had taken for granted. The lovely house they live in, the money in her purse, is all due to Andrew's income and generosity. Andrew is the head of his department. The status that gives her means she can hold her head high when she talks about her husband. She could even put up with the amount of time he spends shut away in his office if they shared a bed, if they had a reasonable sex life.

Pattie sits in the car as motionless as a statue. Dylan is showing Ben how the bike's brakes work. Both boys get up from the ground, then Dylan bends over and pulls the bike into a standing position, holds it still as Ben grips the handle bars and climbs on to it. Ben puts his foot on the pedal and presses down. Dylan lets go and Pattie watches Ben make a shaky journey towards the garden wall. A movement catches Pattie's eye and she looks from Ben to the kitchen window. Linda is putting her head through the open sash; she calls Ben's name then disappears back inside the room. Pattie looks at Ben. He has almost reached the wall; Dylan is running behind him. A flutter of yellow takes Pattie back to Linda. She is in the garden, her bright yellow dress a blaze against the wilting foliage as she hurries towards the boys. They stop what they are doing to look up and listen to what she is saying.

Pattie's hope that she will escape being seen by Linda crumbles when Linda's eyes meet hers. Linda gives a wave and starts to walk towards the drive. Pattie puts on a smile, opens the door and gets out of the car.

'I'm trying to prise Ben away from the bike,' says Linda. 'We really must get going. By the way, your hair looks nice; it suits you.' She looks back at the boys. 'They've been as good as gold. Did you have a nice day?'

'Not really. I would have been back earlier, but I couldn't get an appointment for this morning. I've been in the hairdresser's all afternoon. They over-booked. I had to wait hours. It's not the place to be on a day like this.' Pattie turns away from Linda, ducks her head into the car and retrieves her bag. She closes the door behind her then asks, 'What about you? Did you have a good day?

'Yes, Roberts let me finish early,' says Linda as they leave the drive. 'But time's just flown by. Brian will begin to wonder where we are.'

They stop at the edge of the lawn. 'Thanks so much for having Dylan,' says Pattie, 'but there was no need to hang around waiting for me.' She looks towards the house. 'Where's Andrew? He's quite capable of looking after Dylan.'

'He was in the kitchen. I think he went upstairs; he said he had work to do. But it was my fault we stayed. I wouldn't have stopped, but the boys were enjoying their game and Andrew made coffee.'

'You must have made a good impression. He doesn't usually make coffee for my friends.'

Sensing a hint of anger in Pattie's voice, Linda hurriedly explains, 'Oh, he had started making the coffee before we arrived. He's invited Ben to come and play during the holiday. Is that okay?'

Pattie smiles, 'Of course. Dylan would love to have him round.'

Linda looks across at Ben, 'I really must get that boy.' She goes over to him, then, ignoring his protest, she takes the bike from him and gives it to Dylan, saying, 'Thank you for letting Ben ride your bike; he's had a lovely time.' She stares at Ben. 'What do you say Ben?' Ben puts his hand in hers, sniffs back the start of a tear and whispers, 'Thanks Dylan.' Linda turns back to Pattie. 'Brian will be starving. We must get back. We'll see you at school in the morning.'

Pattie points towards where the car is parked. 'Go out through the drive; it's quicker,' she says.

Pattie waits until Linda and Ben are out of sight then looks over at Dylan. He has pushed the bike onto the patio; she walks towards him and asks, 'Did you enjoy the park?'

He nods and climbs onto the bike, saying, 'I can ride better than Ben.'

Pattie watches him pedal his bike the length of the garden path then calls, 'I'm going in now. Put the bike away when you've finished.'

After the bright sunlight and the activity in the garden, the house seems dark, the silence almost oppressive. When she goes into the kitchen, the first thing she notices is that two mugs have been left on the table. She picks them up. They are almost full; the coffee in them is still warm. The sound of Andrew's step coming down the stairs makes her turn her back to the door. She walks to the sink and pours the coffee away.

She hears him come into the room, his voice telling her, 'You got caught then. I wondered how long you were going to stay in the car. Did she ask what you'd been doing with your time? Did you tell the truth, or did you tell her you'd been at the hairdresser's all afternoon?'

She turns to look at him. 'If you were a proper husband I wouldn't need a lover, I wouldn't have to lie. I don't know how you expect me to live the life of a happy contented housewife when a fundamental thing is missing from our marriage.'

'If you hadn't been so demanding we could have worked something out. You made it quite clear that you thought I was a failure and a disappointment. If you'd shown a little patience, we might have managed to please each other.'

'A little patience! Jesus, Andrew, I wanted to put a bit of spice into our marriage. The weekly missionary position had become a bit of a bore. If I'd known wanting a bit of sexual variety would cause impotency I might have decided to put up with the little I had.' She takes a deep breath. 'I'm sorry; I shouldn't have said that. What's the point? Anyway, Dylan will be in soon, we mustn't argue in front of him.'

'It's my fault. What you do with your time is your business. It's just that I felt sorry for her. She's the innocent in all this.'

'What about me? I feel like an innocent. When I married you I never thought I'd have to look for someone to take over what you should be doing.'

'I've told you, if you're not happy, I'll play the part of the philanderer and you can have a divorce. You won't want for anything.'

'What about Dylan? We have to think of him. He needs a home with two parents; I don't want him to have a part-time father.'

'A part-time father, or mother, is better than two who are either quarrelling or not talking. Think about it; you'll have the freedom to do what you want. Have whoever takes your fancy.'

'You mean like I do now?

'Yes... like you do now.' Andrew takes a deep breath then says, 'It was seeing her at the door; I felt I was colluding with you.'

'If you felt like that why did you invite her in?'

'I don't know; I fancied a bit of company.' He shrugs his shoulders. 'Maybe I should have taken Dylan and let her go.'

She looks out of the window. Dylan is riding his bike in a circle around the garden. She turns back to Andrew, 'If it wasn't for Dylan, I'd take you up on your offer. But we do have Dylan; surely you want to be with him as much as I do?'

'Of course I do. I just wish we could find a solution.'

Pattie leaves the window and sits at the table. 'What do you think of Linda?'

'She seems nice enough.'

'Do you find her attractive?'

'Yes, very; why do you ask? What are you getting at?'

‘I thought someone like Linda, someone not worldly, an innocent as you call her, might be able to help you over this mental block; which is what it is, Andrew. You’ve told yourself so often you can’t get an erection your cock believes it.’

Andrew takes a deep breath and goes to the door.

‘Don’t walk away. Please... sit down and listen to what I have to say. Dylan will be in soon.’

He stops at the door; stands looking at her. ‘I can hear what you have to say from here.’

‘Brian’s interested in wife-swapping. We both think...’

‘What about Linda? What does she think?’

‘Listen to me. My bet is that if the right man was put in front of her she’d....’

‘Has Brian discussed it with her?’

‘I don’t know. I do know he wants to wife-swap. I’ve become quite friendly with Linda. I’m sure with a little encouragement, with the right sort of man, someone considerate, she won’t say no.’

‘What makes you think she’ll like me?’

‘She will. Take Dylan to school in the morning. Linda will be there; get to know her. While you’re with Linda, I’ll catch Brian. I know roughly what time he leaves for work. I want to get him to go to the school play. When the play finishes, I want him and Linda to come here for drinks. We’ll put the boys in front of the television; we grown-ups can get comfortable in the lounge. We’ll see what happens, there’ll be no pressure. You said you find Linda attractive; if she feels the same about you, well, who knows what might happen.’

They hear Dylan in the hallway. Pattie stops speaking. Andrew steps aside as Dylan bursts into the room, saying, ‘I’ve put my bike away. I’m starving.’

‘I thought you had something to eat in the park,’ says Pattie.

‘That was ages ago.’

Chapter 6

Holding tightly to Ben's hand, Linda strides along the pavement. 'I don't want to go home,' whines Ben. 'You're going too fast.' For a few minutes, Linda slows her pace; then, worried about the time, she puts on another spurt.

They are only a few hundred yards from Royal Crescent when Linda spots Brian walking on the opposite side of the road. Anxious that he is out looking for her, and what that will imply, she stands still and waves to attract his attention. She thinks he hasn't seen her and then he suddenly turns and looks at her. Even with the passing traffic zooming between them she can read his anger. 'Wait there,' she tells Ben, then, dodging the traffic, she rushes across the road.

Before she reaches him, before she can get her breath back, Brian shouts, 'Where the hell have you been?'

'I took Ben and Dylan to the park.'

'Do you know what time it is?'

'I'm sorry. I didn't realise it was so late. I had to take Dylan home. Then Dylan wanted to show Ben his bike and...'

'I don't want to listen to your fucking excuses. I've just done two days' solid hard graft. That cab was like a bloody oven; the least you can do is put a meal on the table.'

'I'm sorry. We're here now. I'm going to make a corned beef hash; it won't take long and...'

'I don't want bloody hash. I'll go where I can get something decent to eat.'

'Brian, I...'

She watches him march away, then looks across the road to where Ben is standing. His eyes are focused on her; his feet are at the very edge of the pavement, inches away from the traffic. She indicates to him to move back from the road; then, seeing a space between two cars, she rushes over to him.

Ben's face, his whole demeanour, has changed. When she'd told him it was time to leave Dylan and go home, the boy in the park, the boy who had learnt to ride a bike that afternoon, shrank, closed in on himself. She crouches down beside him, takes his hand in hers. 'Daddy's letting me off from cooking today,' she says. 'He's going somewhere else to eat. We've a few hours to ourselves, just you and me.'

Brian's work clothes - a pair of grubby jeans and a denim shirt, have been left where they fell on the bedroom floor. She picks them up and drops them into the dirty linen basket. The music from Ben's favourite television series "Lost in Space" is coming from the sitting room. She leaves the bedroom and opens the door; Ben's eyes are glued to the screen. 'As soon as it's finished, turn it off,' she says.

She goes into the kitchen, takes the opened tin of corned beef from the cupboard, lifts the lid and looks inside; the corned beef is almost melting. Hoping it might last another day, she tips the corned beef from out of the tin into a ceramic pudding bowl, covers the bowl with a saucer and puts it into a saucepan of cold water. From another saucepan of water, she takes an opened bottle of milk. There is just about enough to pour Ben a drink. She sniffs the milk and empties it into a beaker. The milkman will deliver another pint in the morning.

The sound from the television stops. Ben walks into the kitchen and she gives him the beaker. While he's drinking, she picks up a flannel from a dish on the draining board and rubs it with soap. Ben puts the beaker onto the table, looks at Linda waiting with the flannel in her hand and goes over to her. He grimaces as she wipes his face. 'That's better,' she says. She looks at his hands, wets the flannel again and wipes them, saying, 'After you've cleaned your teeth, put your pyjamas on and bring me "Where the Wild Things Are".

Linda has lost count of the times she has read Maurice Sendak's story about a naughty boy called Max who leaves his home and sails away to a far-off island inhabited by wild scary-looking creatures. Ben has never grown tired of listening to the story; Linda has never grown tired of holding Ben in her arms while he looks at the pictures. The first time she read it to him, Ben had cried; he wanted to know why Max couldn't stay on the island with the Wild Things. She told him it was because his mummy would miss Max even more than the Wild Things would. Linda is glad that Ben is what Brian calls a softie; she doesn't want him to be the model of his father.

When Linda reaches the end of the story, she puts the book aside. Ben is sat on her lap. She looks down at him: his head is resting against her shoulder; his eyes are closed. She cradles him in her arms, carries him to his bed, puts the sheet over him, and gives him one last kiss before quietly closing the door behind her.

Without Ben to distract her, Linda's anxiety grows. She knows from experience that when Brian is angry with her, it is not easily forgotten; he will be looking for any excuse to have a row. If she knew what time he will walk through the door she would be able to plan her evening - she really should catch up with the writing group homework. But she has to be careful. She'll do whatever she can not to irritate him. In her dressing-table drawer is a birthday present from her mother, a box of rose-scented bath cubes, a small luxury that she can only enjoy when she is alone. When Brian is at home, the last thing she wants is perfume on her skin.

Linda turns on the television. David Nixon is performing a magic trick with a handkerchief and someone's wristwatch. Nixon's voice, the audience laughter, jars, makes her go to the screen and switch it off. She takes a library book from the shelf and looks at the title, 'The Female Eunuch". She opens the book, reads a few paragraphs, then flips through the pages. The words are meaningless. She snaps the book shut, wonders what sort of world Germaine is living in. Doesn't she know a married woman's rights disappear as soon as the ring has been put on her finger? She puts the book back onto the shelf and looks at the clock; it's not yet nine, far too early to go to bed, but at least she'll be out of the way when Brian comes in.

The bedroom window is open, but the heat from the day is still trapped inside the small room. She removes her clothes and drapes them over the dressing-table chair - if Brian wasn't sharing her bed tonight she would have slept naked. She takes a brushed nylon night dress from under her pillow, pulls it over her head, pushes each pearl button through its buttonhole until it reaches her neck.

It is still light when she moves the sheet and gets into bed. She lies on her back and stares at the ceiling, waiting for the room to darken. She tries to cast her mind back to the day's events: the escapade of the carpet, the picnic in the park, but a picture of Andrew standing at the window keeps coming to her. The desire to join him, to stand next to him, had been overwhelming and she begins to wonder if his quiet ways, his startling blue eyes had reminded her of her father. She admits she finds Andrew attractive, realises such thoughts should be dismissed; but, unwilling to let them go and taking them with her, she closes her eyes and turns on her side.

A fierce glare of light penetrates Linda's eyes. The pull of the sheet, and she is awake. Brian is in the room. He throws the sheet aside and leans towards her. She brings her knees to her chest; then, aiming for Brian's stomach she straightens them. He falls against the wall.

'You bitch!'

He grabs her ankles, pulls them apart. His weight keeps her pinned to the bed. He pushes himself into her and she gives a cry of pain. She thinks about Ben asleep in the room next to them, stares up at the ceiling as she waits for him to finish.

Chapter 7

Pattie waits a few minutes then rings the bell again. She's beginning to think no one is going to answer when the door partially opens. Eyes rheumy with age peer at her. The door opens a little wider and Pattie looks down on the ancient face of a woman who, from Linda's description, could well be Mrs Jones. 'Yes?' says the woman. Her voice has such an affirmative tone, it would defy anyone to believe that little old ladies are a walkover.

'I've come to see...' Pattie is about to say Brian, then changes her mind, '...Linda.'

'She's not in,' says the woman. Although the woman is no more than five feet tall with the bones of a starving sparrow, her face holds the eye of an eagle.

'Is Brian home?' asks Pattie.

'He's probably getting ready for work.'

'Can you give him a shout? I want to give him a message.' Pattie hastily adds, 'To give to Linda.'

'I can tell Linda. She'll be back from taking Ben to school soon.'

Suddenly Pattie panics. 'No. It's okay. It's not important. I'll see her some other time.'

'What's your name? I'll tell her you called.'

'No. It's alright. I'm sorry I troubled you.'

Pattie turns away from the door. Feeling the woman's eyes on her, she starts to walk along the terrace. She stops with the sound of the door shutting, and hurries to the railings. Leaning over them, she looks for Brian's van. It is parked at the far end of the road. Anxious to be out of sight when Linda appears, she casts her eye for a place to hide.

With its frontage of railings, and the backdrop of Georgian houses, the crescent might as well be a stage. Pattie looks at her watch. Her car is only a short walk away. If she leaves now, she can get the car, park it as close as she can to Brian's van, and wait for him there. She is about to make a dash for it when the sound of the door opening takes her eyes back to the house.

Brian is looking at her open-mouthed. He pulls the door closed, marches over to her, grabs her arm and pushes her along the terrace, whispering, 'Was that you making that racket?'

She pulls her arm from out of his grasp. 'You're hurting me!'

'What the hell are you up to? Stay away from here. Mrs Jones is a nosey old bitch. She loves to know what's going on. She'll sniff out gossip if it was held by the Gestapo.'

He strides ahead of her. Pattie runs to catch up with him. 'It's alright. I told her I wanted to speak to Linda.'

'Why do you want Linda? You know very well she's out. You could have spoken to her at the school.'

'It was a ploy. It was you I was after. I want to talk to you.'

He gives her a puzzled look. 'Me, why? Whatever you want to say could have been said yesterday.'

Wishing he would slow down and listen to her, she hurries to keep up with him. He bounds down the terrace steps, takes a bunch of keys from his pocket and strides towards the van. When she catches up with him, he is about to climb into the cab; she quickly grabs his hand and says, 'Brian, stop for a minute. I need to talk to you.'

'You're not pregnant, are you?'

'No, of course not. I've something to say that could suit us both.'

He opens the cab door, climbs inside, and looks down at her. 'I can't talk now. I'm late. I've got to pick up a load. I'll be about an hour. I'll see you in the usual place. Wait for me there.'

Pattie watches Brian drive away then walks to the car, thinking about Andrew. He's bound to want to know how her meeting with Brian went. When he left to take Dylan to school this morning, he asked what time she would be back. The question spoke volumes. He didn't usually concern himself with when she would arrive home or who she'd been talking to. Well, he'll have to wait; she's not about to jump to attention just because he has decided to speak to her.

Andrew's sudden interest in Linda brought a fleeting moment of jealousy. Pattie knows she is taking a gamble, but what else can she do? Her inability to arouse Andrew sexually has cost time and money: the frequent trips to Ann Summers, the flimsy underwear, the sex aids and whatever else the manufacturer said would improve her sex life, had got her nowhere. The tears, the arguments, the sulking did nothing but drive him away from her bed into the narrow single bed where he sleeps in his study.

Pattie's head tells her she has no reason to worry. Linda may be attractive to look at, but Andrew would soon grow tired of her. They have nothing in common, intellectually, culturally or in any other way. Which is why Linda fits the part she wants her to play so perfectly. Hopefully, with Linda's help, Andrew will recover from his sexual phobia and their marriage can resume in the way most marriages do these days. Perhaps, if things work out well with Brian and Linda, they'll carry on swinging with them. After all, injecting a bit of variety into a relationship is good for all concerned.

Pattie has been parked waiting for Brian for almost an hour. There was a small scrap of shade when she arrived, but now that has disappeared. All the car doors are open, but still the heat is unbearable. She is beginning to wish she had gone home, or at least into a café to use the toilet, her bladder is full to bursting. Desperate to relieve herself, she gets out of the car and looks around her. As usual, the place is deserted. She and Brian have been to the lane at least half a dozen times and only once has she seen another vehicle. She leans into the car, tucks her bag under the seat, gets out and closes and locks the doors. Nearby is a stile to a field, but the sound of a tractor makes her look at the scrubby bushes and untended trees that edge the lane. Holding her skirt tightly in front of her to stop it getting snagged, she fights her way through a tangle of stalks, thorns and dried out foliage.

The spot she finds is secluded but no bigger than a postage stamp. She lowers herself to pee, then mentally cursing and moaning about the brambles, the overhanging twigs and branches and the stones in her sandals, she pulls her pants back into place and stands up. She brushes the dry leaves from her skirt, tells herself she will never put foot on the grotty, sleazy, only fit for prostitutes and one-night stands lane again. She claws her way out of the bushes, steps into the lane and sees Brian saunter towards her. She waits for him then asks, 'Where's the van?'

He takes a drag on his cigarette, then throws the stub onto the ground. 'There's a problem with the brake. Nothing too serious, but it'll take a good hour.'

She unlocks and opens the car doors. 'I was beginning to think you weren't coming,' she says. 'I needed a pee so desperately I was about to go home.' She gets into the driver's seat. He sits beside her. 'It's fucking baking in here,' he says.

'You don't have to tell me,' she says. 'I've been here over an hour. How did you get here?

'One of the drivers gave me a lift. What do you want to talk about?'

'Wife-swapping.'

'Wife-swapping! I told you, Linda's not interested.'

'She might be if it was someone she likes.'

'Why does she have to like him? Anyway, knowing my Linda, and from what you've said about Andrew, it'll be a complete waste of time; sexually, they seem to be as useless as each other.'

'That's why it's a good idea. Swinging improved the Cooks' marriage. They hadn't had sex for nearly a year before they started wife-swapping with the Mitchels. Do you know Karen Mitchel? No, of course you don't. Anyway, from that day on, Carol and David's relationship improved enormously. She told me sex with David is better than it's ever been.'

'Does that mean when you and Andrew get your sex life back I'll be redundant? Perhaps I'd better start picking Ben up from school, do a bit of trawling round the playground. What's Karen Mitchel like?'

'Not your type; she's like Linda, skinny and small breasted. What attracted you to Linda?'

'All my mates fancied her. It was a bet: a fiver for the first bloke who had her. I won. She was a virgin. There's something nice about knowing you're the first one in there. Once I started, I couldn't stop. I assumed she'd go on the pill. I didn't realise how stupid she was; we'd only been together three months and she told me she was pregnant. Christ, what a price to pay.'

Pattie recalls Andrew's dismay at 'having to get married', and his occasional condescending murmur about making the best of it. A moment of sadness washes over her, and she says, 'It's no use complaining about what happened in the past. We can all make changes, and swinging's a good place to start. Or are you worried Linda and Andrew might run off together?'

'Course not; why would she do that? She's got Ben to look after. I don't know about Andrew, but I can't see Linda running off with anybody; she's not the type.'

'The last thing I want is to lose my husband. What I can't understand is why you're so reluctant to wife-swap.'

'It's doing it with you and Andrew. I can't see what's wrong with us carrying on the way we are.'

'Well, I don't like this place. I bet there're all sorts of creeps hanging around. When I went for a pee I worried about the car, worried someone might be creeping up behind me.' She leans towards him, kisses his cheek, puts her mouth to his ear and whispers, 'I want you in my bed. I want to spend a night with you. You won't be disappointed, I promise.'

He puts his hand on her breast. 'Alright, you win. I'll talk to her tomorrow. Though I don't hold out much hope; she can be stubborn.'

She moves his hand away and sits up straight. 'Don't say anything yet. They need to get to know to know each...'

'What's getting to know each other got to do with it? I told you, Pattie, I don't want this turning into a bloody romance.'

'Neither do I, but from what you've said, I guess Linda needs a bit of persuasion. It's the school play on Friday. Tell Linda to get you a ticket. I want to invite you back for a few drinks.'

He puts his hand back onto her breast. 'Okay, okay. I'll go along with it.' He pulls her to him, runs his finger around her nipple saying, 'What you doing now?

'I've nothing planned.'

He moves his hand from her breast and slides it beneath her skirt.

'Not in the car,' she says.

'There's always the bushes,' he says.

'I've already got scratches on my legs. The ground's rough and...'

'Don't be a bore. I'll be the mattress; you like it on top. And I am coming to the play.'

'And I'm probably giving you a lift to the van.' She opens the car door. 'Alright, as it's the last time in this place, a farewell rough and tumble out in the open seems fair enough.'

Chapter 8

After talking to Mrs Jones and thanking her for looking after Ben, Linda climbs the stairs, wondering why Pattie had come to the house. It had to be Pattie; Mrs Jones' description of the woman at the door fitted Pattie perfectly: the height, the hair colour, the Irish accent. What puzzles Linda is why Pattie didn't wait and say what she had to say in the playground. It's all so odd. She stops on the first landing and puts the two heavy bags of shopping she is carrying onto the floor; she takes a few moments to rest against the banister and think about this morning's strange events.

When Linda arrived at the school gate, Andrew was standing on the pavement as though waiting for someone. She and Ben rushed past him: there was no time to stop and talk – yet again, she was late. The playground was empty, the children long gone inside. She'd given Ben a quick kiss and watched him run into the building. When she left the playground, she hadn't expected Andrew to be there still; she couldn't believe he was waiting for her. As soon as she came through the gate he'd smiled and together they walked step for step along the pavement as though it was the most natural thing in the world. She'd been conscious that her hair was uncombed, that her work clothes were stained - in her hurry to finish in the chemist, she'd dropped a glass bottle; the liquid that was inside left a vivid violet mark on her skirt and by the time she had swept and deposited the broken glass she was eight minutes late. When she got home, there was just about enough time to collect Ben from Mrs Jones and run. It wasn't only her hair and clothes that made her feel unattractive. She looked as she felt; tired and depressed by a situation she was unable to change. The continual round of anxiety whenever Brian was at home had taken its toll, replaced any positive thoughts she once had with ones that said the odds were against her, the future grim.

She picks up the bags and walks up the next flight of stairs. It's not the bags nor the heat that make the climb to the top of the house so hard - it's the flat and what happens in it. Knowing Brian is away tonight doesn't disperse the memories it holds, nor does it wipe away the knowledge that he will be with them again tomorrow.

She reaches the top of the stairs, puts the bags down and takes the key from her purse. In the kitchen she lets the bags fall with a thud to the floor. She sits down, watches the potatoes and onions roll across the lino while her mind focuses on Andrew. The walk with Andrew from the school, the congenial conversation, saying goodbye, was over far too quickly. She wonders if Pattie realises how lucky she is. She can't imagine Brian being interested in what teacher Ben is having next term; whether the park in the square needs play equipment or is better left as it is with the rope swing and a natural wildness about it. Her opinion seemed to matter to Andrew. She was pleased when he agreed with her that climbing trees, seeing a few wild flowers and weeds gave the children a small taste of the countryside. She even went as far as to tell him about her writing course. He was interested; he asked her what she was writing about. He made her feel that what she was doing was worthwhile. When they got to Andrew's house, they stood outside talking for a while, then he said he had to go in as he had work to do. She was disappointed. She'd been hoping he would invite her in for coffee.

She forces herself to stand up from the chair, steps over the bags and the vegetables. Hoping a cup of coffee will revive her, she fills the kettle and puts it on to boil. She hadn't slept last night. After Brian had finished with her, when she heard his snores, she went into the sitting room. The small cottage sofa wasn't made to be slept on, but anything was preferable to having Brian next to her. As Linda rinses a mug, she catches sight of herself in the shaving mirror. God, she thinks, what a mess. Brian was right when he said what an ugly depressing bitch she is.

Throughout the morning, Pattie and Andrew are never far from Linda's thoughts. She continues to wonder why Pattie had called at the house. When she thinks about Andrew she is reminded that kind and decent men are around - her father and his gentle ways; Mr Roberts who pays her a decent wage and sends her home with little gifts for Ben. Reminiscing puts Linda into a more positive mood; mid-day she has a sandwich with Mrs Jones. From there, she goes to the library to spend an hour with the writing group. The walk to school, the thought that Andrew might be there, puts a spring in her step. She goes into the playground and casts her eye around, looking for him. She spots Pattie; disappointed and a little ashamed, she puts on a smile and walks over to her. 'Pattie,' she says, 'Mrs Jones told me a woman called to see me. Her description fits you; was it?'

Pattie turns away from the woman she's talking to. 'Yes, it was me. I wanted to invite you and Ben round for a drink after the play finishes.'

Linda is mystified. 'But why go to the house when you knew you'd be seeing me here?'

'Well, I was passing,' says Pattie. 'So I thought I'd call in.'

Before Linda has time to reply, the children come rushing out of school and Pattie disappears. Linda is about to go and look for her, when she decides it is all too complicated, that the best thing to do is forget the matter.

The following day, Linda has another surprise. Brian asks her to get him a ticket for the school play. She is so astonished she wonders if there is another agenda going on.

Chapter 9

The school hall has been buzzing with the chatter of parents and relatives. Now people are settling into their seats, the noise begins to fall. Pattie stands up and looks behind her. Most of the chairs are now taken. A few stragglers are coming through the door, but Brian and Linda are not amongst them. Disappointed, she sits down. If they don't come soon the play will have started, she thinks.

Pattie hasn't seen Brian since the day she'd knocked on his door. She's only spoken to Linda a couple of times. The first was the embarrassing moment when Linda questioned her as to why she had called at the house. Pattie couldn't deny she'd been there; she should have known her accent would give her away. She told Linda she called to invite her and Ben for drinks when the play finished. Then Linda wanted to know why she couldn't have waited and told her in the playground. Luckily the children started coming out of school, which allowed her to escape with Dylan before Linda could waylay her again.

The second time Pattie and Linda spoke was when Linda apologised for dashing off before replying to Pattie's invitation, and that she and Ben would love to call in for a drink. And then she asked if it was alright if Brian joined them, as he was coming to the play.

Andrew has put his jacket on the chair next to him; Pattie's bag is on the chair next to her. If they don't arrive soon, someone would want the seats. Again, Pattie stands and looks behind her. At last; she gives a wave, then beckons them over. They are a handsome couple. Brian's blonde head is a beacon above everyone else's; as he comes nearer, she follows the line of his body. She notices the open buttons on his red shirt, the stretch of white denim pulled tight against his crotch. She looks at Linda; the purple velvet bell-bottoms she is wearing make Linda's legs appear longer than ever. Linda once told her she buys curtains from jumble sales to cut up and turn into clothes, and Pattie wonders if Linda had designed and made the bell-bottoms herself. The white satin blouse she is wearing isn't a choice Pattie would have made, but the contrast with Linda's dark hair is quite striking. Her lipstick, as red as a pillar-box, is an unfashionable colour, but on Linda it has brought a dash of glamour.

They stop when they reach the row where Andrew and Pattie are sat. People stand to let them through. 'Shift along,' says Andrew to Pattie; grudgingly, she picks up her bag and does as he asks - she had hoped Brian would sit next to her. Andrew moves onto Pattie's seat and Linda sits next to him. Linda leans forward, gives Pattie a smile and says, 'Thanks for saving the seats; Brian was late getting home from work.'

'I was beginning to think you weren't coming,' says Pattie; she cranes her neck to look at Brian. 'I'm glad you could make it.'

He is just about to reply when the Headmaster walks onto the stage. They sit back into their chairs. A hush falls across the audience as he starts to speak. 'Ladies and gentlemen...' He looks around the packed hall. 'My, what a crowd. The children will be thrilled to see so many of you here. They've worked extremely hard; they've given up play times, taken short lunch breaks.' He loosens his tie. 'I wish we could do something about the temperature, but other than opening all the windows... Well, I don't have to tell you. There's no interval; we thought you'd want to get out as soon as possible. Anyway, I hope you're sitting comfortably. Let's get on with the show. I'm proud to present...' The curtains begin to open. 'Alice Through the Looking-glass.'

'Alice' has been on stage since the play began. Pattie envies her parents, seeing their daughter performing with such confidence must be such a blessing. Dylan was in tears when he left for school; he was convinced he would forget his lines. She can only hope he's not getting a panic-attack!

She wishes she could remember the story, that she had some idea when Tweedle-dee and Tweedle-dum will appear. A whole host of characters have come and gone: kings, queens, chess-pieces, children wearing masks in the shape of birds, animals and flowers. Hoping to get a glimpse of Dylan, she tries to peer into the wings, then the curtains close. Pattie waits in anticipation. When they open, Dylan and Ben are on the stage. They are dressed in black jackets, stuffed to make them look fat. Each has an arm around the other's neck. Pattie's heart bursts with pride when Dylan says to Alice, 'If you think we're wax-works, you ought to pay.' A lump comes into her throat as she watches him. She's never considered herself to be sentimental, but her eyes are moist, her heart bursting with pride. Both boys are brilliant, Dylan only marginally better than Ben. When they run off stage, she has to restrain herself from standing up and cheering.

Once the boys have played their part, Pattie's mind begins to drift. When they get home, she will tell Andrew to take Brian and Linda into the lounge; he can make them comfortable while she sits the boys in front of the television. When the boys are engrossed in what they're watching, and she's supplied them with drinks and snacks, she'll join the adults. She wonders how the men will get on. Andrew and Brian have nothing in common, but neither has she with Linda. What will they talk about? Not that it matters; long conversations are not to be encouraged. Linda might be a problem. Brian says she is as cold and rigid as an icicle, which is why she plans to ply Linda with more than a fair share of alcohol.

Pattie's mind goes one step further. She'd read in the local paper that a Bistro has opened near the city docks. It said it is 'an intimate place with a bohemian feel'. If all goes well tonight she will book a table. It will be the perfect place to meet; it is unlikely that anyone they know will venture anywhere near the docks.

Pattie's thoughts take her to Andrew and she turns to look at him. His face is glued to the stage. She can't see Linda's profile, but her velvet clad legs are leaning away from Brian's white denim; they are much closer to Andrew's grey corduroy. Pattie looks back at the stage. She has completely lost track of the story. Alice is now talking to Humpty Dumpty, but why and how he got there Pattie has no idea. She watches the characters come and go, all the time wishing the play would come to an end. She senses it is near when Alice and the queens start arguing. Suddenly, for a reason that Pattie has missed, the queens and their entourage run off stage. Alice is now alone. She picks up a toy cat. 'Your Red Majesty shouldn't purr so loudly,' she tells it. Pattie wonders if the rest of the audience are as much in the dark as she is. When the cast take their bow and the Headmaster finishes thanking the audience for coming, she claps her hands as much for the relief of standing up from the hard chair, as pride in her son's performance. The curtains close. It's a shame the leading role was female, thinks Pattie; Dylan would have made a brilliant Peter Pan.

People are starting to leave. Linda is saying something to Andrew, then she looks at Pattie, 'What do you think? Shall we wait for the boys here?'

‘I must get some air,’ replies Pattie. ‘We can watch from the door. I don’t think they’ll be long. The teachers will want to get home as much as we do.’

They join the group of parents standing at the open door. Brian opens a packet of cigarettes, offers one to Andrew, then he turns to Pattie. Admiring his act of assuming she smokes, she shakes her head. Brian takes a lighter from his pocket, holds the flame to Andrew, then lights his own cigarette.

Pattie looks at Brian. ‘Are you glad you came?’

He blows cigarette smoke into the air before saying. ‘Yes, but I could murder a drink.’

‘Hopefully they won’t be long. I’ve put a few beers in the fridge. We’ve wine, or spirits if you prefer.’

‘A beer sounds good; I like whiskey, but I’m not fussy, I’ll drink whatever’s given to me.’

Pattie smiles. They’ve never discussed their preference for food or drink. They’ve never discussed anything that wasn’t sexual. She finds the prospect of a social evening with Brian intriguing.

She looks at Linda. ‘What about you? What would you like?’

‘It’s so long since I had a drink, I can hardly remember what it tastes like.’

The sound of children’s voices makes them look towards the stage. ‘Here they come,’ says Pattie.

A couple of men are stacking chairs; they stop what they’re doing as the children swarm across the hall. Within seconds, Ben is flinging his arms around Linda’s waist, asking, ‘Did you like it?’

‘It was fantastic.’

‘I didn’t forget one word,’ says Dylan, looking from Pattie to Andrew.

'I knew you wouldn't,' says Pattie. 'You were great.' She bends down and hugs him.

Andrew puts his arm around him. 'Well done, son.' He pats Ben on the back. 'Well done both of you.'

'Did you like it, dad?' asks Ben.

'I did; every minute. Now, let's get out of here. We can have this conversation later.'

'We'd better hurry,' says Pattie to the boys, 'there're things on television you might like to watch.'

The boys push their way through the swarm of people leaving the school. Pattie puts her arm through Andrew's as they squeeze into the crowd and follow the boys. She can't remember the last time she had put her arm through his and wonders if she's made a declaration of ownership. They leave the school grounds and she looks behind her to see if Brian and Linda are still with them. For some reason, it pleases her to see them walking a breadth apart. The boys run ahead, then they turn a corner and are out of sight. Pattie takes her arm from Andrew's, saying, 'I'd better go and let them in.'

Pattie is already adjusting the picture on the television set when Linda walks into the room. Ben looks up at her from a nest of toys, saying, 'Dylan's got a colour telly.'

'So I see. Don't get too cosy, we don't want to carry you home.'

'There's a camp bed in Dylan's room,' says Pattie, 'and Dylan has pyjamas he can wear.' The boys' faces light up, and Pattie says, 'So that's it, you're staying the night. What about some snacks? You must be hungry; do you like Coke, Ben?'

Linda follows Pattie out of the room. 'I'll give you a hand.'

'I can manage. I won't be long. Go and join the men.'

As soon as the boys are happily munching on crisps with their eyes fixed to the television screen, Pattie leaves them and goes to the lounge. She opens the door. Brian is sat on the sofa; he appears to be the only one of them who's noticed she's entered the room. Linda is sitting in the small club chair next to the window; Andrew is standing talking to her. Pattie guesses that Andrew is asking Linda what she would like to drink. Interrupting him, she says, 'Linda, have a gin and tonic, it's the perfect drink for this weather.'

Linda turns to look at her. 'I don't know… I mean, I don't think I've ever tried gin… perhaps a small one.'

'What do you mean, a small one?' says Brian. 'A bit of alcohol won't hurt you; you might even start enjoying yourself.'

'Don't worry,' says Pattie. 'I'll put plenty of tonic in it; you'll hardly taste the gin.' She turns to Brian. 'What about you?' Without waiting for a reply, she goes to the cocktail cabinet, takes out a glass and a bottle of whiskey and gives it to him. 'I'd have thought you'd have the drinks sorted out by now Andrew,' she says. She looks at Linda and shrugs her shoulders. 'He leaves everything to me.'

She hurries out of the room and goes into the kitchen. When she comes back she is carrying a tray holding a bucket of ice, a bottle of tonic water, a sliced lemon, and two bottles of beer. Andrew is sat in his favourite chair, sipping at what looks like whiskey. Three long tumblers have been put onto the coffee table; Pattie puts the tray down next to them. 'Help yourself to beer,' she tells Brian, 'and don't let Andrew hog the whiskey.' She pours herself and Linda a large measure of gin, adds tonic, ice and lemon, then passes Linda her drink. Taking hers with her, she sits down beside Brian. 'We won't hear a peep from the boys,' she says. '*Some Mothers* is on, then it's *Morecambe and Wise*.' She raises her glass. 'Cheers, everyone.'

There's a moment of silence, then Andrew says, 'What did you think of the play? I was struck by how much work has gone into it. Not just organising the children, but the costumes and scenery. How did they manage to put on a play as well as run a school?'

'They had a lot of help from some parents,' says Linda. 'John Turner's mother works for a theatre company; she managed to borrow the backdrops. Jo Smith makes and designs clothes for a small boutique; she had a lot of off-cuts and made the costumes.'

'They must have a hell of a lot of time on their hands,' declares Brian. 'What do you think, Andrew? All these women with nothing better to do than mess around with a kids' play?'

Pattie knows that Andrew wouldn't usually give Brian the time of day. She looks from Brian to Andrew, wishing that this particular conversation hadn't started.

Andrew closes his eyes as though giving his answer some thought. 'I looked after Dylan when Pattie was in London and quite enjoyed it. I don't mind watching him when Pattie's out, but I know she'll take over when she gets home. I wouldn't want to be tied to the house. I leave Pattie to do the housework and the shopping. In fact, I think men have the best of all worlds.'

All three of them are looking at Brian, waiting for his answer. For a moment he looks uncomfortable, then bravado steps in. 'I think a woman's place is in the home,' he says. 'That's the way it's always been. Men go hunting and women cook the food. My dad went to work, and mum looked after the kids. She had a little cleaning job for pocket money, but she was happy doing what she was born to do. Anyway, I can't look after Ben, I never know what time I'll be back, and at weekends I'm knackered.'

Andrew looks at Linda. 'Do you agree?'

‘I’m glad I was there when Ben was small, but now I’d like to find a job that pays more money, one that I enjoy and fits in with school hours.’

‘What did you do before Ben?’ he asks.

‘Window-dressing, but the hours won’t suit. They’ll want someone to work weekends. Customers usually want something taken out of the window on a Saturday. I wouldn’t mind retraining.’

‘You!’ Brian glares at Linda. ‘Retraining for what?’

‘Pattie jumps up from the chair, saying, ‘Linda, you’ve hardly touched your drink.’ She grabs the gin bottle, goes over to Linda and fills her glass to the brim. ‘I probably put too much tonic in it; try it now,’ she says.

‘Does everybody like Tina Charles?’ she asks as she walks towards a shelf stacked with records. ‘*I Love To Love* is such a sexy song.’ She selects a few LPs, takes them from their sleeves, opens the lid of the record-player and slips them onto the spindle. Moving to the music, she dances towards Brian. ‘I love to love,’ she sings as she takes his hand. She pulls him up towards her. He puts his arms around her waist and they sway to the music. Dionne Warwick starts singing *Walk On By*. Pattie looks at Linda through half closed eyes; she is still in the club chair. Andrew appears to be rooted to where he is sat. Pattie is beginning to think that neither of them will move, when Andrew stands up and walks over to Linda. He says something to her then he takes the empty glass from her hand, puts it onto the table and pulls her up towards him. ‘You’ll Never Get To Heaven,’ sings Dionne. Pattie closes her eyes and rests her head against Brian’s shoulder. The Three Degrees harmonise ‘When Will I See You Again’. Pattie looks again at Linda and Andrew. She puts her lips to Brian’s ear. ‘Take a look at Linda,’ she whispers. ‘I reckon if the kids weren’t here we’d be swinging tonight.’

Chapter 10

Ever since that night, the night of the play, Linda has been asking herself, how did it happen? Was it the amount of alcohol she drank that made her behave in the way she did? Or was it the simple fact that she has been attracted to Andrew almost from the day she first set eyes on him? What she finds amazing is that one minute she was sat alone, feeling ill at ease, wishing she wasn't there, trying hard not to look at Brian and Pattie dancing in a way that was more like a prelude to sex, and then, like a flash from a fairy wand, she was in Andrew's arms. His body against hers, his hand on her buttock, created a sexual urge that can only be described as animal. Without thinking about what she was doing, she pressed her body against his, opened her mouth and they started kissing. It was a good job Pattie had the good sense to turn the sound of the music down and remind them the boys were still watching television. It was after the boys were in bed that they sat together with yet another drink and discussed wife-swapping. It is no good pretending she was the innocent amongst them; she had been as enthusiastic as the rest of them.

Since then Linda has been on tenterhooks. One minute she is restless with excitement, the next plagued with the doubt that she'll disappoint him. Having sex with someone she hardly knows is new to her. Brian's the only man she's been with, and they did have some kind of courtship before they actually did it, even if it was for only a few weeks. Despite the butterflies in her stomach, she has no regrets. The thought of seeing Andrew tonight makes her feel alive, makes her heart beat in a way she would never have expected.

For the last half hour, Linda and Ben's bus has been stuck in traffic. Now the road is clear, it is gathering speed. Linda looks at her watch; it's already gone eleven. Time is being eaten away, and her mother will expect her to stay for at least an hour. She thinks about the number of things that are waiting to be done. As well as the journey home, she wants to call into the Co-op and buy new bed-linen; she had made a resolution not to take on any more HP, but the few sheets she has are threadbare. Then there is the weekend shopping, a pile of ironing, and the beautiful black 1920s dress found in the Oxfam shop that needs a bit of hand stitching. Hopefully, she will find the time to have a bath and wash her hair. She looks out of the window. The junior school she attended comes into view. She taps Ben's hand. 'Come on, we're here,' she says.

The bus stops and they alight onto the street that Linda grew up in. Nothing has changed: whiter than white nets hang at every window; each door is painted the same shade of council green; in front of almost every house is a well swept path and a small tidy garden. Linda's mother's garden looks sadly out of place. Since her father died it has been seriously neglected; the grass is the colour of straw; in the flower beds only dandelions survive: when her father was alive no weed would have dared raise its head. But her parents' roles had been clearly defined. Gloria wouldn't contemplate picking up a trowel, any more than Reg would have touched a saucepan. Linda is pretty sure her dad had never cooked a meal in his life.

Linda and Ben walk through the alleyway that divides her mother's house from her neighbour's. Her mother's back door is open, and they walk straight into the kitchen. Gloria stands up from the Formica table. 'Ben, Linda!' She is wearing a floral-patterned apron; a tin of polish and a yellow duster peeps from her pocket. She comes towards them, bends to kiss Ben, turns to Linda and offers her cheek to be kissed. 'I was wondering what time you'd get here,' she says. She picks a comic up from the table and gives it to Ben. 'I bought you this week's Beano. Would you like lemonade or squash? There's a Waggon Wheel in the cupboard. Put his bag in the sitting room,' she tells Linda. 'Do you want tea or coffee? I've only got Camp.'

'Camp will be fine,' says Linda before opening the connecting door that leads to the sitting room. She closes the door behind her, stops at the sideboard, and picks up a photograph. It was the last picture taken of her father. The last holiday he and Gloria would take together. He is smiling into the camera, looking happy and well, unaware that a tumour is growing inside of him and that in six months from then he will take his last breath. Linda stares at her father's face. She thinks about the night in front of her, what she is about to do, and a wave of shame washes over her. She puts the photograph back onto the sideboard and calls, 'I might as well take his bag upstairs.'

She climbs the stairs and walks into the small, rose-patterned bedroom. She puts Ben's bag onto the floor, sits down on the pink quilted eiderdown and casts her mind back to when the room was hers. What a blessed childhood she'd had. She was an only child but never hankered for siblings. She had everything: new toys, a poodle to take for walks, a tortoise in the garden, a week-long caravan holiday by the sea each summer. She thought being adored would go on forever; she never dreamed it would come to an end. When she walked out of the room wearing a little cream suit and a feathered hat on her wedding day nine years ago, when she registered the disapproval in her mother's tight-lipped stare, the sorrow in her father's eyes, she was convinced they would soften, that they would get to know Brian and love him as much as she thought she did. What a fool she had been.

Her mother shouts up from the bottom of the stairs, 'Linda! Your coffee's getting cold.'

Ben is sat at the kitchen table absorbed in his comic; Linda sits beside him and picks up her coffee. 'What on earth were you doing?' says Gloria, 'That coffee will be cold. Let me make you another.'

'No, it's fine,' says Linda. She takes a sip, then makes a grimace. No matter how often she says one spoonful is enough, Gloria insists on piling in the sugar.

'I know what you're going to say, Linda, but you need the energy. You really do. Though I must say you look a lot better than when I last saw you, a bit more like your old self. Perhaps it's the thought of a night out.' Before Linda can protest, Gloria takes the cup from her hand, saying, 'You can't drink that, it's cold.'

'Where are you going tonight?' asks Gloria as she empties Linda's coffee into the sink.

'Out for a meal with friends. Ben's told you about Dylan. Pattie and Andrew are Dylan's parents.'

'That'll be nice, dear. Your dad and I used to go to that lovely steak house near the Centre; you should give it a try.'

'It's all arranged; Pattie booked a table at a new restaurant.'

'That'll be nice, dear.' Gloria hands Linda a fresh cup of coffee then turns to Ben. 'I've bought you a little present, Ben. It's on the shelf in your room.'

Ben immediately jumps up. 'What is it?'

'You'll have to go and find out.'

Ben rushes from the room. 'It's an Action Man,' says Gloria. 'I know he's been wanting one.'

She fiddles with her cup. 'I worry about you, Linda; you were such a jolly girl. Now, most of the time, you've a face as long as a fiddle. I'm glad you're going out, it'll cheer you up. I'll always have Ben, you know I will. You and Brian are hard workers, but all work and no play makes Jack a dull boy. You need a bit of fun, a bit of romance in your lives. You need to get out a bit. Spend a bit of time together without Ben. It helps keep a marriage alive. Me and your dad were courting till the day he died. Every week we'd do something, even when you were little. Do you remember Mrs Hendy? God rest her soul. She'd watch you while we went out. It could be anything, a walk in the park, a night at the pictures, a drink in the pub. I can see us now, Reg with his pint, me with my sherry. God, every day I miss him, Linda.'

Gloria searches through her apron pocket, puts the duster and tin of polish onto the table, pulls out a pink, lace-trimmed handkerchief, and blows her nose. She looks at Linda, 'I want you to be as happy as me and your dad, Linda. You have to try at a marriage; you've got to work at it. I often wonder how you and Brian are getting on. You never mention him. Even when I ask, you brush it off and change the subject. When you were upstairs, Ben told me Brian went to the play; he sounded really pleased about it. A boy needs his dad. I know you got off to a bad start, being pregnant. But there are plenty of girls that get in that condition. Take Jenny Smith in number 12. She's been married five years; they've two little ones now. Mrs Smith told me they've managed to save the deposit for a house. Brian must earn good money, and what with all your cleaning jobs...' She pats Linda's hand, and stands up, saying, 'What about another cup of coffee?'

'Thanks Mum, but I've things to do. I'll just go up and say goodbye to Ben.'

There are hidden objects under the bedcovers, creating a landscape of lumps and curves. With Ben's help, Action Man is standing on a mountain made of pillows. 'I'm going now,' says Linda.

Ben looks up at her. 'Will you see Dylan?'

'No, we're not going to his house; we're going out for a meal.'

'Where's Dylan?

'I think he's staying with Carol Cook.' Linda bends over and kisses the top of Ben's head. 'I'll see you tomorrow.'

Ben picks up Action Man and lets him drop face down into an eiderdown valley then looks up at Linda. 'He'd much rather be with me than sissy Sally Cook.'

Chapter 11

Pattie and Andrew walk into Green's Restaurant. Before they left the house, they had argued, and she is still annoyed with him. Andrew had wanted to call a taxi; Pattie wanted to take the car. Pattie won, but what she sees as Andrew's attempt at controlling her has made them fifteen minutes late. They stand looking into the dimly lit room; it's far busier than Pattie had envisaged. She casts her eye around the room seeking Brian's blonde head.

'Where the hell are they?' she murmurs. 'They should be here by now. She wonders if they have changed their mind. It was always open to question whether Brian would call it off. Or maybe it was Linda; perhaps she decided against it. She was all for it when she had a quarter bottle of gin inside her; after she'd sobered she might have thought differently.'

Pattie has done her utmost to make this evening happen. If they're not coming, she and Andrew will have to leave. She can't sit at a table alone with him; the journey in the car had been bad enough. They go further into the room, when Pattie spots Linda tucked away in a far corner. Squeezing between loaded tables and chairs seated with diners, they make their way towards them. Linda and Brian are sitting opposite each other. Linda has picked up the menu and is looking at it. Brian is gazing around the room with a bored expression. They look up when Pattie says, 'I'm sorry we're late. I hope you haven't been waiting long.'

'We were a few minutes late ourselves,' says Linda.

Pattie puts her bag onto the floor and sits down. Brian indicates a bottle of wine and the four bottles of beer in front of him, saying, 'The waitress should be along any minute with something to open them with.'

Andrew takes two bottles of wine from a brown paper bag, places them on the table, then sits down. 'It's a novel idea letting you bring your own,' he says.

Pattie looks from Linda to Brian, saying, 'If Andrew had had his way we'd have only brought one bottle. He has a thing about drinking and driving. I told him I drive better after a drink or two; better still after three or four.'

'I suggested we call a taxi,' says Andrew.

'This is what I've got to put up with,' laughs Pattie. 'Mister cautious, worried I might drive into a brick wall, though he won't learn to drive himself. We were already late. God knows how long we would've had to wait for a taxi! Anyway, I'm hungry. What's this place got to offer?' She picks up a menu, holds it away from her as she tries to read it. 'Jesus! It's dark in here,' she says. 'You'd think it was the middle of the night.' She looks around her. The walls are painted a deep olive green; red velvet curtains almost cover the arched windows. A few table lamps with dark brocade shades struggle to shed even a glimmer of light; candles in wax-encrusted wine bottles flicker on every table. Pattie points to the candle in the middle of their table. 'Very bohemian,' she says, 'but it's as useless as a torch is to a blind man.'

'You should have brought your glasses,' Andrew tells her.

Pattie shoots him a threatening look. 'I've told you, I can see perfectly well without them.'

A waitress wearing a black see-through blouse appears. She puts a corkscrew, a bottle opener, four wine glasses and a beer mug onto their table. She smiles at Brian. 'Let me know if there's anything else I can get. Call me when you're ready to order.'

Brian watches her as she moves to another table. He looks at Andrew. 'This summer's definitely brought out the best in women. Did you notice she's not wearing a bra?'

Andrew turns to look at the waitress.

Feeling agitated with both Andrew and Brian, but trying to keep a smile on her face, Pattie puts her hand on Brian's arm. 'Are you going to open that bottle?'

Pattie not only finds it difficult to read the menu, choosing a dish has become equally challenging. 'Do any of you know what... God, how are you supposed to say it? It starts with G, third one down.'

'I think it's pronounced as Goulash,' says Andrew.

Linda turns to look at Pattie. 'I've heard of it, but I don't know what the ingredients are. I might have the nut roast.'

Pattie puts the menu flat onto the table. 'Nuts are for Christmas, though at least you'll know what you're eating, even if you can't see what you're putting in your mouth.' Then, leaving choice to fate, she closes her eyes and puts her finger on something called Moussaka. She sits back into her chair. 'I don't know what I've chosen. I'm not even sure if I can pronounce it, so I'm none the wiser as to what it is, but, for the sake of my eyesight, I'm going to have it. When the waitress takes the order, I'll show her the menu and point at it.' She sits back into her seat, saying, 'I wish someone would have the sense to open an Irish restaurant. I tell you, a bowl of boiled bacon and cabbage, or a plate of colcannon and fried eggs, and you'd be hooked.' She looks around the table. 'Has anybody else chosen?' She turns to Brian. 'What about you?'

'There's nothing here I fancy.' He puts the menu down and calls over to the waitress. She had been on her way to another table, but she stops and makes her way towards him. Standing far closer than necessary, she asks, 'Have you decided what you're having?'

He looks up at her. 'What I want isn't on the menu, but, getting back to food, I'd like to know what I'm supposed to be eating. There's nothing with the word meat written on it.'

'There's minced beef in the lasagne, and lamb in the Moussaka. They both come with a salad.'

'They sound foreign to me, and I bet there's garlic in it. I can't stand the stuff. As for salad, you can leave that to the rabbits.'

'Well yes, I'm sorry, there's garlic in most courses, though I don't think there's any in the nut roast; that comes with roasted vegetables. I'll tell you what I'll do, I'll get the chef to get some minced beef out of the fridge; he'll make you a burger in next to no time. If you would like me to, I'll tell him to give you plenty of roast veg.'

'You're an angel, and a beautiful one at that.'

She looks around the table. 'Anybody else ready?'

The last of the wine has been poured into the glasses. The tension that had lingered across the table is now diffused. They've discussed the food and agreed it was surprisingly good. Andrew had ordered dairy-free chocolate cake. He had given each of them a small piece to taste when they didn't believe how delicious it was. They had complained about the weather; Pattie and Linda had discussed ways of keeping the boys entertained during the long hot days. Throughout the meal, Pattie has been aware that one particular topic of conversation has been avoided: the reason why the four of them are sat around this table, the venture they're about to embark on, has been deliberately not spoken about.

Pattie has grown tired of the idle chit-chat. They've done the social niceties. Now the prick of jealousy when she sees Andrew listening attentively to Linda's every word is beginning to hurt. She wants to get on with what she came for and go home. Again, she looks at Andrew; Linda is saying something to him and he smiles. Pattie looks from Andrew to Brian. Brian's eyes are following the waitress. She taps his arm. 'Are you ready?'

Brian takes his eye from the waitress. 'Yeah, let's get out of here.'

She looks back at Andrew and interrupts the conversation he is having with Linda when she says, 'We'd better get the bill.'

Pattie has parked her car near to the restaurant; she unlocks the car door then turns to look across the road. Andrew and Linda are walking along the pavement. Pattie turns back to the car when she hears Brian say, 'Aren't you going to let me in?' When she looks again, Andrew and Linda have disappeared, have gone into the lane that leads to Royal Crescent, and Linda's flat.

Chapter 12

Linda and Andrew hadn't noticed Pattie watching them from the other side of the road. Now they have turned into the lane, they are out of her sight. It's a steep climb to the top of the lane, and there are few street lights, but a full moon has made the sky translucent, has cloaked their path in a soft silver hue. The air is balmy; white roses clambering over an old stone wall, a pot of night-scented stock in a small courtyard has created a heady concoction of perfume. The clank from a dustbin lid, the howl from a cat fight, a woman's voice singing from an upstairs window are like fanfares in the quiet air. But Linda is unconscious to the sounds and scents of the night; all she perceives is Andrew's step next to hers, his breath as they climb the hill, the brush of his shirt sleeve against her bare arm. They stop for a minute to look down at the docks; the restaurant has disappeared from view; the buildings have become mere pinpricks of light.

Linda has been longing for this moment, has dreamed of how it will be when they are alone together. Now that moment is here she doesn't know how to behave. Whether she should take his hand, if she should she put her arm through his.

'You're sure you want to do this?' His voice startles her and she turns to look at him. 'You don't have to have sex if you don't want to, you only have to say.'

'Don't you want to be with me?' she asks.

'Yes, I do, but we don't have to have sex if you're not comfortable with it.'

'But I am,' she says as she slips her arm through his.

The lane has an air of seclusion, as if it is a secret place that is theirs alone. When they reach the top of the hill, when they step from the lane onto the pavement, Linda feels suddenly exposed. The traffic on the road hurtles past them. A throng of people, laughing and chatting, merry from a night out, monopolise the pavement. She takes her arm from his and they walk quickly through the crowd. They stop at Linda's door and she puts her key into the latch. 'We must be quiet,' she whispers. 'Mrs Jones lives on the ground floor; she's probably in bed. I wouldn't want her to hear us.'

Andrew follows her into the house, stands aside as she silently closes the door behind them. She feels for the switch and the naked bulb lights their way up the stairs. They stop on the landing. She flicks another switch, puts her mouth to his ear. 'Not much further.' At the top of the stairs, she points to the bathroom. He shakes his head. She opens the door to the flat and they step inside. 'It's very small compared to where you live,' she says as she takes him to the sitting room. She turns on the light and draws the curtains. 'Not that anyone can see us, we're that high up. Take a seat,' she tells him. 'I'll put the kettle on. I've no coffee, is tea alright?'

Leaving the kettle on the gas ring, she goes back to the sitting room. Andrew is sat on the sofa. He looks out of place, uncomfortable, more like a patient waiting to see a dentist, than a man who is about to have sex with her. 'How many sugars?' she asks.

She makes a fuss of putting the little table near to him. She asks if his tea is sweet enough, does he want more milk?

'Aren't you having a drink?' he asks as she sits down beside him.

She shakes her head. 'No.'

'Are you okay?'

'Yes, a little nervous, that's all.'

'Don't be, not of me. I told you, you don't have to do anything if you don't want to.'

'But I do want to,' she says. 'It's just... It's just it feels strange. I've never done anything like this before. Brian's the only man I've been with.' Remembering the rumours she had heard in the playground, she asks, 'What about you? Wife-swapping, I mean. Have you done it before?'

'Yes... once.'

'Who was it with?'

'Friends of Pattie's.'

He takes a few sips from his mug and she wonders if he is as nervous as she is. She touches his fingers, puts her hand around the mug and places it on the table. She turns towards him, leans forward, is about to kiss him, when he says, 'Are you on the pill?'

'I've a coil.' The question reminds her of the reason he is here; she must face the fact that love, or even a romance, is inconceivable. She tells herself swingers want variety; that this will probably be their one and only night together. She won't spoil it by hankering for the impossible; she will make a memory to cherish, and asks, 'Shall we go to the bedroom?'

He stands up. 'I'll use the bathroom first.'

'We share the bathroom,' she tells him, 'you might have to wait.'

As soon as Andrew leaves the flat, she hurries to the bedroom. She switches on the bedside light, undoes the buttons on her black lace dress and steps out of it; she throws the dress across the chair as though it were nothing more than discarded wrapping paper. Rushing to get into bed before Andrew comes into the room, she pulls off her underwear then, leaving a puddle of peach-coloured nylon on the floor, she slips under the sheet.

'How many people use the bathroom?' he asks as he comes into the room. 'I didn't bring pyjamas.'

Holding the sheet to her breasts, she sits up and points to the hook on the door. 'You can borrow Brian's dressing gown if you need to.' He starts to undo his belt. Still holding the sheet to her breasts, she turns onto her side, listens to the sound of his clothes being removed, the pad of his bare feet as he moves towards her. He climbs in beside her; she leans over him and turns off the light. Feeling less shy now the room is dark, she loosens her grip on the sheet, rests her hand on his shoulder and puts her lips to his.

Andrew's butterfly kisses, the way he has stroked her skin as if she were a child, have aroused Linda to such a point of excitement she feels she may burst. She had expected his kisses to engulf her, to feel the weight of his body on hers. She thought her role was to be naked beside him, to let him touch her where he wanted, to open her legs when she felt his need. She realises, with Andrew, it is not the case, that something more is needed. She puts her hand onto his leg, strokes his skin in the way Andrew had stroked hers. She moves her hand to his thigh; her fingers touch his mat of pubic hair and... He pushes her hand away, saying, 'It's no good.'

'I'm sorry. I'm not...'

'It's not your fault,' he says, removing his arm from around her. He turns onto his back. 'I can't do this; it's all so contrived. I can't turn it on like a tap.'

'But you've done this before, you told me, with a friend of Pattie's.'

'With Carol Cook, a while back; it was a disaster. Pattie should have warned you. I swore I wouldn't do this again. I don't want to be part of the swinging crowd, but Pattie insisted... and... I found you attractive, and well, here we are. I must be a great disappointment to you.'

'No. I don't mind. Really, I don't. I thought it must be me, that I wasn't doing enough. That I'm to blame, not you. Is there anything you'd like me to do? Could we...'

'No. There's nothing.' He moves up the bed, sits with his back against the headboard. She reaches across him to turn on the light. He takes her hand. 'Leave it, I like the dark.' She sits up beside him. 'What made you agree to do this?' he asks.

'You,' she says.

'Me...?'

'Yes, you. I remember the first time I spoke to you. It was in the school playground. After that, I was always looking out for you, hoping to bump into you.'

'If I'd known, it would have boosted my morale no end. I'm flattered. Though, as you've discovered, I'm no lover.'

'Brian says I'm frigid. I thought so myself. I'm not sure if I ever enjoyed sex, though, I suppose I must have when I first met him. Being with you has made me think differently, especially the night we danced. I didn't want that dance to end.' She strokes his cheek, 'If you want to, we can try again.'

He shakes his head. 'No, not tonight. I'd rather talk. I want us to get to know each other.' He puts his arm around her and she rests her head on his shoulder. He tells her about his early life in the two-up, two-down cottage on the Yorkshire Moors. How proud his parents had been when he got a place at university, the relief his father expressed when he knew his only son would not be going down the mines, like the generations before him. He describes the moors with such passion, she can feel the vastness, the wildness of it, can see the hills and dales, the huge sky.

'Where did you meet Pattie?' she asks.

'In Ireland. My grandparents came from a small village on the West Coast. My mother always wanted to see where her parents grew up. When dad died of emphysema, and mum's health was deteriorating, I thought, now's the time to go. So, we went to this tiny place in County Clare. I met Pattie in the bar of the pub where we were staying. We exchanged addresses. I thought I wouldn't see her again, then she wrote and told me she was pregnant. It was a shock; we only met a few times. If only she'd told me she wasn't... though I should have guessed. Pattie was a young single woman living in Ireland; any form of contraception was almost impossible to get hold of. Mum didn't get to see Dylan; she died of a heart attack before he was born.'

There is a pause in the conversation, then Linda tells him about the death of her father and how much she misses him. How lucky she is to have a mother who is so helpful with Ben, who would give her last penny to her if she needed it. She describes her lovely childhood, the treats and holidays her parents gave her. She doesn't tell him about her marriage, her plan for a future without Brian.

Light begins to filter through the curtain. Linda looks across Andrew to the bedside clock. 'What's the time? How much longer do we have?'

He turns to look. 'It's 6.30; we still have a few hours.' They lay face to face. He strokes her hair, runs his finger down her nose, traces the shape of her lips. 'I'm sure you've heard this all before,' he says, 'but you're very lovely.'

'Dad called me his lovely girl. He used to say, "You'll have the pick of the bunch, our Linda." That was a long time ago. When I look in the mirror now I see shadows under my eyes and hollow cheeks. Brian tells me I'm too thin, and he's right.'

Andrew moves the sheet aside, looks at her naked body. 'I think you're perfect.'

Linda touches her breasts and smiles. 'I could do with a bit more here.'

'Twiggy and The Shrimp wouldn't be where they are now with big breasts,' he tells her. 'What about Botticelli's *Three Graces*? You may have seen them depicted on greetings cards. They're Aphrodite's hand maidens. Botticelli painted them dancing hand in hand. If he'd painted them with big breasts flopping around, they wouldn't have been called the Three Graces.' She laughs. 'I mean it,' he says. He kisses her, then says, 'I want to do this again, soon, perhaps next weekend.'

Linda smiles. 'Yes, next weekend. Mum's always happy to have Ben. I'm sure Brian will be all for it. He's been trying to get me to agree to wife-swap for ages.'

Chapter 13

Pattie opens her eyes, raises her hand to block out the light that is streaming through the window. The curtains are wide open. The sky is clear blue; it's going to be another hot day. Already the air in the room is at blood heat. Her head is thumping, her tongue as dry as flaking paint. Hoping to find a forgotten drink of some sort, she raises her head and looks on the bedside table; all she can see is an empty bottle of whiskey. She is naked. The sheet that had covered them has fallen and is now lying somewhere on the floor. Brian is next to her, snoring loudly.

Her head falls back onto the pillow and she closes her eyes. It takes an age to go by before the grogginess, the thump in her head, starts to fade. As her mind clears she begins to remember coming in from the restaurant. It must have been about eleven-thirty. They hadn't hung around downstairs. They didn't bother with cumbersome glasses when they grabbed the three-quarters full bottle of whiskey left on the kitchen table. From the kitchen, they climbed the stairs and made their way to Pattie's bedroom. They had fallen onto the bed, drank whiskey straight from the bottle, had sex in a hundred and one different ways. She can't remember what time it was when they finally rolled away from each other.

She looks at Brian; is loathe to wake him. Sleeping with him, seeing his long body curved on the mattress, has made her realise how much she misses having a man in her bed. Waking each morning to smooth, undisturbed sheets, to the empty space on either side of her, is like being marooned, magnifies the fact that she is on her own, that Andrew left her bed because he doesn't love her, doesn't desire her in any way.

A picture of Andrew and Linda in bed together imprints her mind; she thumps the mattress with a closed fist, as though the enactment playing in her head can be broken apart. She reminds herself that she was the one who planned and coordinated what happened last night. Reviving Andrew's interest in sex had been paramount to her, thinking that it was the one way to bring him back to her. She hasn't changed her mind; she is still convinced that when Andrew's libido is in working order, she will be able to rekindle the feelings he'd once had for her.

She thinks back to the evening she first saw him. She had been working in the local bar, he came to the counter and she served him drinks. He took them to a table where an elderly woman was sat. She'd been immediately attracted to Andrew. It was not only his good looks that drew her attention: his accent was not Irish. She was desperate to get away from Ireland, away from her narrow-minded parents, their prayers, Holy Water and Saints' days. She wanted to escape from the claustrophobic feel of the village. Andrew had a kind face. She thought he might know of a job going in England, or a place where she might stay. She was working as a general dogsbody in the pub. Andrew and his mother were staying in a couple of the upstairs rooms, so she had had plenty of opportunities to get to know him. She flirted with him, and one thing led to another. It came as a surprise to discover he was a virgin, not that she was that experienced. The local lads had been lectured so often by the priest as to what would happen to them if they touched a girl before marriage, they would not go near one. Pattie's only sexual encounter had been when she went to London with a girlfriend for the weekend and met a soldier on leave. She lost her virginity behind a bush in Hyde Park. She had felt very worldly when she seduced Andrew; he needed a bit of encouragement, but that had been all part of the game, made it all the more rewarding when Andrew wanted more of what she had to offer and started chasing her.

Brian has stopped snoring. Pattie turns to look at him; his eyes are still shut, his breathing is softer and more regular. She pushes herself up, rests herself against the headboard, acknowledging the huge differences between Andrew and Brian. She knows only too well that Andrew will never satisfy her sexual needs - the missionary position would soon become repetitive and eventually bore her to tears. She admits that life will be a drag without variety, that she thrives on a little danger and an adventure every now and then. Having a lover has not taken her love from Andrew, and she can honestly say their marriage has been far from terrible. Andrew is a kind and loving father who takes his responsibilities seriously. He gives them security, financially, and in every other way. What surprises her is that, despite complaining about his lack of libido, she is finding more and more that she is longing for his touch. She recognises she is more than partly to blame for the rift between them and realises she will have to control her temper. She admits to herself that it does no good comparing Andrew with Brian because the fact is she needs them both.

She glances at the clock; it is 9 o'clock. Andrew and Brian had agreed to leave for home at ten. She touches Brian's cheek, says his name and his eyes open. 'You'd better get up,' she tells him. 'Andrew will be home in less than an hour. If you want breakfast you'd...'

He turns onto his back, stretches his arms, then he grabs her around the waist and pulls her to him. 'Bugger breakfast,' he says.

She watches Brian as he pulls on his jeans. 'What a night,' she says. 'I don't know why we haven't done it before. Do you think Linda's mum will have Ben next weekend?'

He fastens the buttons of his flies. 'We're not doing it again.'

She looks at him in surprise. 'Why not?'

'Because I don't want to, that's why.'

She stands up from the bed and walks over to him. 'What's the matter?'

He pulls his T-shirt over his head. 'Nothing. I just don't want to do it again.'

She puts her hand on his shoulder. 'But we had such a great time. You enjoyed it as much as I did. What's the problem?'

He slips on his shoes. 'Swapping. I don't see the point in doing it with you and Andrew. You and I have always managed a fuck without having him and Linda involved.' She waits for him to tie his shoe laces, then he stands up, saying, 'Swinging's about variety. There's a whole load of women I'd like to get my hands on. Take Carol Cook, she looks fun. Anyway, if Andrew's going to fuck my Linda on a regular basis it could lead to complications.'

'What do you mean?' she asks already knowing the answer.

He shrugs his shoulders. 'Who knows? They might get to like each other. And we don't want that, do we. You need Andrew as much as I need Linda. He's your meal ticket, and if my Linda gets it into her head to run off with somebody, who's going to cook my dinner?'

Chapter 14

After they kiss goodbye and Andrew leaves her side, Linda stands at the top of the stairs watching his descent. She is naked under her dressing gown, her bare feet feeling every crack in the linoleum. He reaches the first landing, looks up at her, smiles and waves; then he turns the corner to the next flight of steps and disappears from view. She doesn't move as she listens to his footsteps gradually getting fainter as he makes his way to the ground floor. The distant sound of the front door opening and closing behind him brings their time together to a full stop. She still stands with her hands on the banister, still stares down into the empty stairwell as though some miracle will bring him back to her. The door to the flat is behind her; it is wide open. The thought of going through it fills her with unease. If she knew that a relationship with Andrew will be allowed to develop, if she was sure she will see him again, just the two of them, she would turn to the door and walk into the flat counting the days. But the possibility of them meeting again hangs in the air; one word from Brian could blow away any hope of being with Andrew again. She knows she must be careful. The last thing she wants is to arouse suspicion about her true feelings for Andrew.

Realising time is ticking away, Linda hurries into the flat, closes the door behind her and goes into the bedroom. The black lace dress she wore last night is draped across the chair. She picks it up, takes it to the wardrobe and puts it onto a hanger. She gathers together the peach nylon bra and pant set from the floor, pushes them into her dressing table drawer and assembles a random assortment of underwear. From the chest of drawers, she takes a pair of old jeans and a T-shirt and puts them on. She is about to go to the kitchen when she decides to take a last look at the room.

She wants the room to be clear of any sign that Andrew had been with her - the night had been for them alone. While Andrew was getting dressed, she'd picked up the sheet from the floor, thrown it over the bed, pulled the corners straight and smoothed away the creases. She hadn't touched the pillows; hadn't noticed the impression of Andrew's head on the pillow where he had lain. Remembering Andrew's touch, the shape and feel of him, she walks back into the room, picks up the pillow and holds it to her cheek. Brian's head will be on that pillow tonight. She puts the pillow back onto the bed; the one that Andrew used is now on her side.

She takes a quick look at the bedside clock; Brian will be home at any minute. She leaves the bedroom and rushes to the kitchen. Her intention is to go through the day in her usual complaisant way, to continue letting Brian carry on with the illusion that she is willing to be subservient and is happy to cater for his every need. She will try to keep the smile from her lips, show no sign that something rather special happened last night.

She takes the frying pan from the shelf and spoons a lump of lard from the fat basin into the pan. The smell of bacon frying always pleases Brian. The fat is beginning to sizzle when she hears him come into the flat. She takes two slices of bacon from their greaseproof wrapping and drops them into the pan. She doesn't take her eyes from the frying pan when he walks into the kitchen. He stands behind her; she stiffens a little when he puts his hands onto her shoulders. 'Great,' he says. 'Just what I need; chuck an egg in there.'

She relaxes when he moves away. She hears him pull out a chair, pictures him sat at the table with his legs folded as he watches her every move, as he looks for a sign that will tell him how her night with Andrew went. She picks up an egg, is just about to crack it into the pan when he says, 'Next time, we'll try another couple.'

She breaks the shell of the egg and says, 'What do you mean?'

The egg falls into the pan. 'What do you think I mean?' he says. 'Can't you understand plain English? I said, next time we'll try another couple. That's what swinging's about, variety. We need to spread our wings, put a bit of spice into our life. Christ, we don't want to carry on swapping with those two; we might as well be married to them!'

She flips the bacon over, turns the egg to give him the sunny side up that he likes. 'We didn't have sex,' she tells him.

'You what...?'

'We didn't have sex.'

'Why not...?'

'He... I... We ended up talking.'

'Talking! For Christ's sake, last night wasn't about talking. What a moron. What about you? Couldn't you get it up for him? There are ways to help men that can't get a hard on. If a hand job won't do it, you could always give him a... but, of course, you wouldn't, would you, you're such a prude, Linda. Pattie was telling me how dead her marriage is, they don't even sleep together. I told her mine's not much better.'

'We were nervous,' she says as she uses the spatula to stop the food from sticking to the pan. 'Next time will be easier; we'll feel more comfortable with each other, I promise. If we do it with another couple, I'll worry it will fail again. I didn't try hard enough; I was shy. You know what I'm like. Next time will be different.' She puts the food onto the plate, carries it to the table and puts it in front of him. ‘How many slices of bread?’ she asks.

‘Three. God, Linda. I should have guessed you’d be bloody useless. Okay, we’ll do it with them again. But whether you manage it or not, this is the last time. I don’t care what you say, I’m going to be finding us another couple. Get me a knife and fork, and where’s the ketchup?’

Chapter 15

Pattie looks at the clock. Andrew should have arrived home a good hour or so ago. 'Where the hell is he?' she mutters. She swipes at a fly; her fingers knock a ceramic milk jug that had been holding the few dandelions that Dylan had picked from the garden, and it falls from the window ledge. The sound as it hits the floor, seeing the puddle of water, the flowers and pieces of broken crockery spread across the tiles, make her want to cry. Not that the flowers, nor the jug, had any sentimental value. The dandelions had been wilting for the past couple of days, and there are plenty more of them in the garden; they seem to manage very well in the scorching heat and despite not having a drop of rain for what now must be well over a month. As for the jug, if she was asked where it came from, she wouldn't remember if it was Woolworths, or any other such place. The fly continues to buzz around the room. Conscious that it's not the breakage nor the fly that has upset her, she wipes away a tear, opens the kitchen cupboard, takes out a dustpan and brush, then kneels on the floor. Absorbed by the events of the morning and a feeling of helplessness, she sweeps the pieces into the pan.

When she and Brian got back from the restaurant the previous night, everything had been perfect; they both enjoyed having the comfort of a bed and used every minute to indulge in just about every sexual fantasy they could think of. She had expected Brian to be as enthusiastic as she was about the four of them swinging again, would never have guessed that the following morning he'd say he wanted to find another couple, that he couldn't see the point of doing it with her and Andrew when he's screwing her anyway. He refused to listen to her argument, didn't seem to care that she would find it difficult to meet him during the school holiday, ignored the fact that she really didn't like the seedy lane and the van's hard grubby floor. She'd ended up getting extremely annoyed with him, had been a hair's breadth away from saying she didn't want to see him again, when, as though he hadn't heard a word she was saying, he put his arm around her, kissed her cheek and walked out of the room, whistling "A Hard Day's Night". The next thing she heard was the slam of the front door.

After he left, after she calmed down, she started to think that perhaps it was all for the best, that maybe the moment of panic when she saw Andrew and Linda cross the road after leaving the restaurant was a warning, the scenario playing through her head a preview of what could develop between Linda and Andrew. It was impossible to predict what mood Andrew might be in when he arrived home; it would probably depend on how successful his night with Linda had been. But whatever mood he is in, she will tell him straight away what Brian had said. She might even say that perhaps it was a good thing, that Linda and Brian were probably the wrong sort of people to play such games with. Whatever happens, she promised herself she will remain calm and in control.

She empties the dustpan into the bin, then she notices that the fly is now on the wall above the cooker. Feeling the fly is going out of its way to annoy her, and not wanting the disgusting creature to get the better of her, she takes her eye away from the fly and concentrates her anger on Andrew. It was agreed between the four of them that the men would aim to leave for home at ten. If Andrew had other plans he should have told her. Weighed down by a feeling that everything is against her, she sits at the table wondering if he could possibly be with Linda. She shakes her head. He wouldn't take that risk. Anyway, Andrew is a stickler for rules; he knew he had to be gone before Brian arrived back home.

She hears the front door open. The sound of Andrew's footstep coming towards the kitchen causes her temper to rise. When he walks into the room she stands up from the table. 'Where have you been? Brian left hours ago!' She stares at him. He looks tired; he stifles a yawn. She notices the relaxed way he takes off his jacket, a sort of nonchalance when he hangs it on the back of the chair. The look on his face, the slight rise in the corner of his mouth that says a smile is just a second that away, triggers her to boiling point. 'Jesus, Andrew, just fecking answer me,' she shouts.

He sits down. 'I didn't realise you'd be waiting. I went for a walk and sat in the park for a while. I was going to ask if you'd had a good night: it seems you didn't.'

She glares at him. 'I had a grand night.'

He leans back into the chair. 'That's good. What time do you want me to get Dylan?' he asks.

'There's no hurry,' she tells him.

'Well in that case...' He stands up from the chair.

'Where are you going?' she asks.

'To my room. I thought I'd have a nap before getting Dylan.'

'I want a word with you.'

'What about?'

'Last night.'

'Do I have to report back to you?'

'I don't need to know the details. You look tired. She must have done something to keep you awake. I knew she would. The trouble with you, Andrew, is you can't handle a real woman. They scare the life out of you.'

Andrew walks towards the door saying, 'Call me when it's time to get Dylan.'

She waits for him to cross the room then says, 'I'm glad you had a good time because it will be the last. Brian doesn't want to do it again, not with us anyway.'

Chapter 16

Brian told Linda that, if she wants them to get together again with Pattie and Andrew, she must make the arrangements herself. Despite her embarrassment, and the shame the words “wife-swapping” and “swinging” bring to her, she knows that if she wants to be with Andrew she will have to be the one to make it happen.

Desperate to talk to Pattie before Brian has time to change his mind, the following morning she arrived at the playground in plenty of time. She stood next to Pattie and they watched the boys go into school; then she followed Pattie through the school gate. As they walked along the pavement, Linda glanced round to see if there was anybody within hearing distance, then, in a low voice, she told Pattie that Brian had asked her to make another date with them and would she and Andrew be free to meet this coming weekend. Linda’s heart sank when Pattie said she was thinking of giving up swinging; then soared to new heights when Pattie suddenly said okay, as long as they gave the restaurant a miss. Linda immediately agreed - she was more than happy not to waste precious time sitting at a table with Brian and Pattie, and they made an arrangement that the men would arrive at their respective houses Saturday evening at 7.30.

Since then, Linda has been in a constant state of anxiety, fearful that everything is going to go wrong, that Brian will change his mind, her mother will become ill and not be able to have Ben, and a million other things that might prevent her being with Andrew. She has nagged herself, told herself over and over again, to relish the anticipation and not let her imagination take her any further than the night that she and Andrew will be together. That she must stop believing that this will be their last night together, enjoy each and every moment she is with him, and not let one pessimistic thought get in the way.

She has made a promise to herself not to worry about the ring of the doorbell, or who may see the strange man come into the house and follow her up the stairs. For once she agrees with Brian that it's their business what they do and who they invite into their flat. Even Brian's constant reminder, 'You'd better manage to do it this time; there won't be a third attempt,' will not spoil their night together.

When Linda lets herself into the house, she rejoices. Ben is now at her mother's, and none of the disastrous events that have played through her mind have happened. She climbs the stairs, walks into the flat and puts the bag of shopping she is carrying onto the kitchen table. As well as a piece of steak for Brian's tea, she has bought a few things to make a meal for Andrew. She has decided to prepare him a salad, as it is something that can quickly be thrown together when Brian leaves the house - she is hoping that sitting at a table and sharing a meal with Andrew will normalise the evening, help take away the emphasis from the main event being sex.

Linda unpacks the bag; her mind is on the conversation she had with her mother. Gloria asked too many questions: ''Where are you going? Is it to the same restaurant? Will it be a regular thing? Are you meeting those same people... Pattie... and what's his name... that's right, Andrew? Are the four of you going out for a meal? Not that I mind. I love having Ben. I'm pleased you've made nice friends.'

It had been bad enough lying to Gloria, but Ben had been in the room and was stood listening to their every word. She had felt his eyes looking through her, as though he saw beyond the words to the lies she was telling. Although it was the start of the school holidays and he was going to be staying with Gloria for the whole week, she'd been so overwhelmed with guilt that all she wanted to do was to get away. She'd hugged Ben, told him to be good, hurriedly gathered together her belongings, garbled excuses and told yet another lie, saying she had an overdue bill to pay at the electric shop and had to get there before they closed. Then she threw them kisses and dashed out of the door.

Linda takes the cheese, lettuce, cucumber and tomatoes from her bag and puts them well hidden into the back of the cupboard; if Brian knew what she is planning to do with the food, she is sure he would confiscate it, but, far worse than that, Andrew would not be allowed to put a foot through the door. She notices the time. Brian will be in the betting shop for at least another hour; she can be bathed and have her hair washed before he arrives home. She goes out onto the landing; glad to see that the bathroom is vacant, she turns on the tap.

The Greco family start playing their guitars. Flamenco fills the bathroom. Enjoying the music, Linda closes her eyes, rests back into the water, and taps her foot on the rim of the bath. It is when the water starts to cool that she wonders what the time is. She pulls out the plug, puts on her dressing gown and picks up her clothes from the floor. When she leaves the bathroom, she sees the flat door is open; quietly, she steps inside. The sound of the television comes from the sitting room. She had completely forgotten the football team Brian supports are playing this afternoon. Trying not to make a noise, she opens the bedroom door. She lays her clothes on the chair, puts her toilet bag into the dressing table and hangs her towel by the open window to dry. She is about to untie her dressing gown when Brian calls her name.

She goes to the sitting room and stands in the doorway. He takes his eyes from the screen and looks at her. 'Getting ready for him, are you? Washing your hair won't get him a hard on.' He gets up from the chair and looks her up and down. He smiles. 'It's a rubbish game. Get into the bedroom; I want to show you a trick or two. This is going to be the last time you and he get together. You'd better start learning how to please a man.'

Chapter 17

Pattie ignores the tap on her bedroom door. When Andrew walks into the room, she remains sitting at her dressing table, looking into the mirror. His reflection appears. She carries on powdering her face as though he isn't there.

Andrew is clean shaven, and his hair is neatly combed. The care he has taken over his appearance makes her regret agreeing to Linda's request, adds another notch into the gradual erosion of their relationship. She has watched their marriage be chiselled away by arguments since Dylan was a baby, and now the gulf between them has grown so wide she feels she is losing him. Unable to bear the sight of his carefully groomed looks, she lowers her face, picks through her make-up bag, then empties its contents onto the dressing-table.

'I'm going,' he tells her. 'I suppose the same set of rules apply. I'll leave Linda's at 10.00.'

Fully aware that he is stood behind her waiting for an answer, she chooses a lipstick, takes her time as she carefully applies the palest shade of pink to her lips. She puts the top back onto the lipstick and over-attentively places it back into her make-up bag. 'Will you be going on another ramble, or will you come straight home?' she asks.

'I don't know. What difference does it make?'

'Jesus, Andrew! It was a simple question. The reason is I don't want to leave Dylan with Carol half the day. If you're not coming back at a reasonable time I'll collect Dylan. Also, and this is for Dylan's sake, the school holidays are on us and we need to do something as a family - the three of us: you, me and Dylan. I'll drive us somewhere.'

‘Okay, if that’s what you want. What do you have in mind?’

‘A picnic maybe. What about the park, or out into the country? We’ll take a ball; a bit of exercise will do us all good.’

‘Yes, as long as we can find a bit of shade. I’m not so sure about games, not unless a miracle happens and the temperature drops. Don’t worry about getting Dylan, I’ll pick him up on my way back, or would that be too early?’

‘No, we could make a day of it.’

‘I’ll see you in the morning then...’

He waits for a moment, as though there is something else that needs to be said. When she picks up her mascara he knows it’s time to go.

The door closes behind him. Pattie puts the mascara down, sits listening to his footstep run down the stairs. The slam of the front door conjures a feeling of jealousy. Andrew’s desire to get away and go to Linda triggers a spark of anger. Not wanting her feelings to get in the way, she casts her mind from Andrew, thinks about Brian and the night in front of her. She grabs a handful of cotton wool, wipes the lipstick from her lips and chooses another colour.

She stands up from the dressing table and walks to the full-length mirror. Dark mascara, grey eye shadow, lipstick as red as a pillar box. Black nylon underwear that clings to her figure, pushes and pulls her shape to where she wants it to be. She picks up a bottle of perfume and sprays her cleavage. ‘For those intimate moments,’ the bottle tells her. If only Andrew could be seduced so easily.

She gave up hoping that Andrew would fulfil all her needs almost from the point when they first met. She knew then that some desires she would to have to satisfy for herself. At the moment, Brian is her stockpile and there was no reason to think that it wouldn’t continue. She enjoyed spending the whole of the night with him in the comfort of a bed, but Brian is right, Andrew and Linda are made of different stuff; it's wise to keep them apart.

Chapter 18

After Brian has finished with her, he shifts his body from hers and Linda folds her dressing gown around herself. She turns onto her side and puts her face to the wall. She feels the rise of the mattress as he leaves the bed and she relaxes a little. She listens to his movements as he straightens his clothes. He is whistling "A Hard Day's Night"; the cheerful notes cut her senses to shreds. She heaves a silent sigh of relief when his steps recede and he is outside the bedroom, and gives a prayer of thanks when the flat door opens then slams. Silence falls like a blessing. She pushes herself up and away from the bed. His semen dribbles down her leg. She grabs her pants from the floor, uses them to try and wipe herself clean, then hurries to the kitchen. She turns on the tap, holds the pants under the cold running water as she covers them with soap and washes between her legs. She scrubs her skin until it smarts, takes the lid off the bin and drops the pants into it.

A sudden weariness overtakes her. She would like to disappear, to fall into a chasm and re-emerge with no taint of Brian's violation. Desperate to sit and rest for a moment, she walks into the sitting room and drops onto the sofa.

Linda opens her eyes; her head is resting on the arm of the sofa. The last thing she recollects is leaving the kitchen to sit down for a few minutes. She moves herself so her head leans against the sofa back. Gloria's words when she told her she was pregnant come back loud and clear. 'You've made your bed Linda, now you must lie on it.' How right her mother was.

She looks at the clock; Andrew will arrive in less than an hour. The excitement that had been with her at the thought of him coming has left, and she has to drag herself from the sofa. She goes into the kitchen and puts the kettle on. While the water is warming, she collects her toilet bag and towel, then washes her face and hands at the kitchen sink. She goes into the bedroom and looks at the sheets; they were clean on this morning. The only other decent set are in the laundry basket waiting to be washed. She pulls the sheets into place then sits at the dressing-table. She looks into the mirror, runs her fingers through her hair, pulls it up into a ponytail then lets it fall loose. She takes a container of mascara from her makeup bag, is about to wet the little brush with her tongue, when she stops what she's doing and examines her face, thinking why waste time; what can a bit of makeup do? If it was able to inject a bit of optimism into her life she would plaster it on. She puts the mascara back into the bag, goes to the wardrobe and opens the door. She had planned to wear a red cotton skirt she'd found in a church jumble sale, but the hem needs attention; the way she feels now, even if she had the time, she would not bother to mend it. She takes out a grey maxi skirt and the cream blouse her mother had given her, puts them on and, without bothering to look in the mirror, she leaves the room.

A part of Linda wishes Andrew wasn't coming, but she knows she will she regret it if she told him to go; she'd also be playing into Brian's hands: his actions were meant to unsettle her.

The sound of the doorbell echoes through the house. Linda's heart takes a leap; her resolve not to care if people see Andrew coming into the house is forgotten when she rushes from the flat. It is on the last flight of stairs that she sees Mrs Jones walking unsteadily towards the door and shouts, 'It's for me!' She slows her pace, produces a smile and says, 'I'll get it: we're expecting a visitor.'

Mrs Jones stands watching as Linda opens the door. Andrew steps into the house. Linda looks at Mrs Jones. The lies are spontaneous. 'Brian will be back soon,' she says. She notices the bottle of wine wrapped in a brown paper bag that Andrew is carrying and says, 'He's gone to buy a bottle of wine. Ben's at Mum's so we thought we'd make the most of it and invite a friend around for a few drinks.' The old lady stands aside to allow them to pass. Linda stops at the bottom of the stairs, turns to look at Mrs Jones and says, 'We won't disturb you; I've told Brian to be quiet when he comes in.'

'Don't worry dear,' says Mrs Jones. 'I'm almost stone deaf. I rely on my eyes to tell me what I need to know.'

'I rely on my eyes; what does she mean?' says Linda, when they go into the flat. 'She suspects. She must do!'

'She probably doesn't,' says Andrew as he follows Linda into the sitting room. 'And if she does, there's nothing you can do about it. It might brighten her day, give her something to talk about. How old is she? She looks pretty ancient. She'll probably have forgotten I exist by the morning.' He puts his arm around her and in a concerned voice asks, 'Are you alright?'

'Just a little anxious.'

'What about?'

She shakes her head and shrugs her shoulders.

'Try not to worry,' he says. 'Next time we meet, we'll make sure it's somewhere where we're not known'.

'There's not going to be a next time,' she says. 'Whether we have sex or not, Brian doesn't want to do it again. Not with you and Pattie, anyway. He wants to try another couple.'

Tears prick her eyes and she moves away from him. She looks out of the window, takes a deep breath before saying, 'But I won't. I only agreed to do this because I want to be with you.'

He puts his hand on her shoulder saying, 'Pattie told me what Brian said. I've been mulling it over. I don't want to stop seeing you; I've been hoping you feel the same.'

Hardly daring to believe what she's heard, she turns away from the window and looks at him wide eyed. 'If Brian finds out, I daren't think what might happen.'

'We'll be careful, I promise. I've got married colleagues that have been having affairs for years. They seem to get away with it.'

She listens to what he says but doesn't reply. An affair for years is not what she wants to hear; she wants more than that. 'What about Pattie?' she asks.

'There are no secrets between Pattie and me. I know she has lovers and who they are. We have an understanding. I don't interfere with her sexual affairs and she won't with mine.'

'But I see her in the playground. What happens then?'

'Nothing; it won't affect your friendship, or the boys. Ben will still come and play.'

'Are you seeing anyone else?'

'No. Other than wife-swapping that one time, I haven't been with another woman. Anyway, where do you keep the corkscrew? I think it's time for a drink.'

'I've bought a few things to make a salad, and there's a steak in the cupboard; Brian went out before I had time to cook it,' she says. 'Though you're probably not hungry.'

'I'm not starving; I had a sandwich before I left. I won't have the steak, but a salad will be nice. I'll give you a hand.' He picks up the bottle of wine and follows her to the kitchen.

As he searches through a drawer, she puts the salad ingredients onto the table. Andrew finds a scout knife with a dozen attachments, opens the bottle and puts it onto the table, asking, 'What can I do?'

She gives him a lettuce to wash. 'Tell me about your life before Brian,' he says.

She takes a knife and commences to cut the cheese into neat little cubes. 'There's not much to say. I went to the local secondary school, left when I was fifteen and trained as a window dresser.'

He leaves the lettuce to drain. 'How long have you and Brian been together?'

She puts the cheese into a bowl and says, 'About eight years. I was pregnant when we married.'

'It's a trap we fall in,' he says. She shakes the drips from the lettuce into the sink wondering if the 'we' he speaks of are all men.

'Where are your glasses?' he asks.

She puts the cucumber she is about to cut down and says, 'I'm sorry; the only glass is a pint mug. I've mugs and teacups. The teacups are bone-china; they were a wedding present.'

He laughs, 'Let it be teacups; they'll help turn what's probably a mediocre wine into something rather special.'

She can tell he is not hungry, but neither is she. They pick at the food and she wishes she'd thought of buying a bottle of salad-cream. He wants to know everything about her, how she and Brian met, what her father did for a living, what schools she went to and her favourite subjects. The picture she paints is dull and unexciting. Her father had a number of jobs, all of them manual. She failed her eleven-plus, didn't excel at anything, was born in the local maternity hospital a stone's throw from her parent's house and lived with them until she married Brian. She wishes there was something interesting she had to say about her life, is embarrassed by what she sees as her lack of intellect and talent. When there is a break in the conversation, she searches for a change of topic, and then he asks if she's thought anymore about furthering her education. She becomes almost tongue-tied; her main hope for the future is to get away from Brian. When he asks to see her writing, she shakes her head, makes excuses; she would rather not let him know how ignorant she is.

Andrew has made no move towards her sexually. She thought, after Brian's attack, she would be the one to shun away from bodily contact. But the longing to feel Andrew's arms around her has been growing by the minute. Without thinking about what she is doing, she gets up from the table. Paying no attention to what he is telling her, she moves to his side, takes the cup of wine he is holding, and puts it onto the table. He looks up at her. She kisses his mouth, takes his hand and leads him from the kitchen and through the bedroom door.

Daylight has flooded the room. Linda and Andrew are naked; they lay face to face, her hand resting on his shoulder; his hand is curved around her waist. The sheet is on the floor. He kisses her cheek. 'I'm sorry,' he says. 'I've let you down again.'

'There's no need to worry,' she tells him. 'Being with you is enough.' Which is not true; she is disappointed. For hours she has tried all she knows to consummate this relationship.

He takes his hand from her waist and strokes her inner thigh. His caress brings another wave of desire and she shifts her body from his. She removes his hand from her leg, rolls onto her back, closes her eyes, breathes deeply to stop her heart from racing. For a minute, they do not speak; then he moves towards her and she feels the weight of his leg slide across hers. She had given up hoping he will achieve an erection, hadn't expected to feel his penis hard and urgent. She arches her body wanting every inch of him inside of her. He gives a cry of pleasure. For a moment he lies still, then pulls himself away from her, saying, 'I'm sorry, I couldn't help myself. I haven't made love for a long time.' For a minute or two, she holds him tightly to her, fearful that if she loosens her grip she will lose him forever. If she could stop time, this is where she will want it to stay. That moment doesn't last long. Andrew moves her arms away from him and pushes himself into a sitting position. 'I suppose I'd better get going,' he says.

She sits up beside him. 'Yes, you'd better. I didn't realise the time. When will I see you again?'

'Whenever you're free.'

'I don't work on Tuesday, and Ben will still be with mum. Brian's working away that night, so I won't have to hurry back.' She doesn't tell him that on a Tuesday, when she has the opportunity, she attends the library writing group.

He tells her, 'There's a pub near the docks called The Coronation Tap. We could meet there for lunch; it's quite close to Green's Restaurant.'

They agree on a time and he stands up from the bed. He picks his clothes up from the floor, and puts them on, saying, 'Pattie's planned a picnic for this afternoon. I'm not sure where we're going, but it'll be good to get out of the city and find somewhere cool.'

Any romantic notion she has that this affair will develop into something serious is suddenly squashed. He and Pattie may have what he calls an 'understanding' and Brian might have been right when he told her Andrew and Pattie did not share a bed, but it's quite obvious that Andrew is committed to his family. Trying to stifle the jealousy that is starting to prick her, Linda throws her legs out of bed. She picks the sheet up from the floor and wraps it round her body, saying, 'I'd better get a move on too; I need to clear the remains of our supper before Brian gets back.'

Chapter 19

Pattie has been sat waiting for Brian for almost two hours. Her body is squeezed into black lace underwear, her breasts pushed in and up so tightly she feels she will carry the lace marks forever. She taps her fingers on the arm of the sofa, and her eyes dart to the window. She tries to ignore the need to keep gazing down the street to see if he is coming, but compulsion forces her up from the sofa and she looks outside. Other than a cat stalking a bird, and an elderly couple about to cross the road, the place is devoid of life. Disgruntled, she purses her lips and goes back to the sofa. She picks up this month's "Cosmopolitan", flips through the pages, inattentively scans an article about women who have never experienced orgasm, then throws the magazine aside. She looks at the clock - he is now two hours and sixteen minutes late. The thought of spending the night alone casts a gloom over her. Any other time she would enjoy having the house to herself, but not tonight, not while Andrew is in Linda's bed. She begins to wonder if Brian had decided to call the whole thing off; he was never very keen on the idea, but then asks herself, if that is the case, why didn't Andrew come home? It occurs to her that perhaps they're having a threesome. She immediately eliminates the thought; even Brian would understand that any sort of orgy with Andrew and Linda would be a complete waste of time. She has arrived at the conclusion that Brian is spending the night with some other woman, when the doorbell rings. Not expecting anyone other than Brian, and unsure whether to be relieved or angry, she deliberately takes her time in answering. She pulls the door open. 'I was beginning to think you weren't...' She can see straight away he is drunk.

He staggers into the house, saying, 'I met a couple of mates and we went for a pint.'

She stands back from the smell on his breath. 'A pint,' she snaps. 'Well over that. I think you'd better go. I don't want you here in this state!'

He leans against the wall and laughs. 'Don't be an old misery. I can't go home; I might spoil whatever Andrew and Linda are up to. Did you think I wasn't coming? Better late than never. Anyway, I'm here, I've got what you want and I'm ready and able to deliver the goods. Where would you like it? Here on the floor? Spread across the kitchen table? What about Andrew's bed? Don't stand there with your gob open.' He pushes himself away from the wall. 'I suppose it'd better be your bed.'

Speechless, she watches him go towards the stairs. He lurches forward and grabs the newel-post to steady himself. Frightened by what the consequence might be if she confronts him, she stands silently watching as he takes hold of the banister and pulls himself up to the top of the stairs. He reaches the landing, and almost falls through her bedroom door.

For a moment, Pattie is so shocked she doesn't move. Her underwear has become increasingly uncomfortable. Now the reason she is wearing it has probably passed, and desperate to remove it, she goes upstairs and into Dylan's room. Cursing Brian, she struggles with the hooks and eyes. Eventually, she pulls the underwear away from her and flings it across the room. Now she is naked, she realises that all she needs - night clothes, make-up remover, moisturiser, hair-rollers - are in her bedroom. Determined to stay away from Brian and not wanting to be alone downstairs, she lifts the sheet and gets into Dylan's bed.

Her anger, her frustration, her thoughts and emotions, have kept her awake for what seems like hours. One minute she is listening for Brian's step, hoping he will come looking for her to apologise; a moment later, she has to stop herself from rushing to her room and ordering him out of the house. Yet again, moving images of Andrew and Linda together, each one more erotic than the last, have played through her head. It is now clearer than ever that inviting Brian and Linda to wife-swap was a bad choice, and she and Andrew must cut all ties with them. She contrives a course of action, rehearses the conversation she will have with Andrew when he arrives home. She will admit there are times when her temper has got the better of her, but he has to accept that he has also been unreasonable. She will convince him how important it is to make their marriage work; how crucial it is for Dylan.

Dawn begins to creep into the room. The long night comes to an end and Pattie welcomes the new day with the hope of a fresh start. She is wondering if Brian is awake, and how she is going to deal with him, when he shouts her name. The sound of his voice causes her anger to flare, and she pushes herself into a sitting position. She pulls the sheet to her and calls, 'I'm in the room opposite you.'

Brian walks into Dylan's room bringing a rancid stink of beer and cigarettes. From the look of them, he has slept in his clothes. And probably his shoes as well, she thinks, as she pictures the dirty marks on her clean Irish linen. He sits on the edge of the bed. His eyes are bloodshot, his skin pallid beneath the summer tan. He puts his hand on her arm, saying, 'I'm sorry about last night.'

She pushes his arm away. 'Get off this bed!'

'Don't be like that,' he says, standing up. 'You know how it is. You meet a few mates and get carried away. Anyway, I've been thinking, perhaps we'd better stop seeing each other for a while. It's been fun, but I think we should move on. I don't want Andrew twigging on that you and I are seeing each other; he might think he can do the same with my Linda. You'll soon get a few blokes lined up to take my place.' He starts undoing the buttons on his jeans. 'Move over; what about one for the road.'

She glares at him. 'I don't want you anywhere near this bed. As for sex, if you were the last man on earth, I wouldn't touch you. You did me a favour. Turning up the way you did made me see you for the scum you are. Now get the feck out of my house.'

He re-buttons his jeans, looks at her and smiles. 'Thanks. I only offered 'cause I felt sorry for you. For your sake, I hope Linda managed to give Andrew a hard-on; otherwise, until some other sucker comes along, you'll have to remain the frustrated bitch you are.'

As soon as she hears Brian leave the house, Pattie carries the vacuum-cleaner into Dylan's room. She is glad she said no to Brian, pleased that their relationship is over. Even if she'd been on good terms with him, there is no way she would have allowed him to get into Dylan's bed. Still furious, she picks her underwear up from the floor and carries it to the bin - all reminders of the previous night are banished. When she is happy with Dylan's room, she goes into her own room. She cleans the dog-ends from the floor, changes the sheets, all the time thinking about and cursing Brian. She asks herself, who does he thinks I am? Some little scrubber picked from the side of the road? Last night he looked dreadful; he certainly showed himself for what he is: a brute with a brain that goes no further than his dick.

She hears Andrew and Dylan come into the house, checks her lipstick, runs her fingers through her hair, puts on her brightest smile and goes down to meet them.

They are in the hallway. She kisses Dylan's cheek. 'Did you have a good time?'

He nods. 'Carol gave me a box of colouring pencils.' He holds the box out to show her. 'You dip them in water and paint. Can I have some water? I want to paint a Dalek; we watched "Dr Who"; it was so scary.'

They follow her into the kitchen, and she goes to the tap, fills a beaker with water and gives it to Dylan. 'Do the painting in your room. We're going out, but first I need to talk to daddy.'

She waits for Dylan to leave the room, then looks at Andrew. 'Would you like a coffee? You haven't forgotten the picnic, have you?'

'No; I don't think Dylan's too keen. He said he wants Ben to come. I told him Ben isn't around and he asked me how I knew. I told him I'd seen Linda and she said he was at his nan's. That seemed to satisfy him.'

'He'll enjoy it when we're there. It'll be good for us as a family. Where do you fancy going? What about the beach? It'll be cooler there, and it's not much more than an hour's drive.'

She picks up the kettle. 'But first, let's have that coffee; I need to talk to you. It won't take long to get a picnic together. Somewhere in this house there's a beach ball and bucket and spades. Could you see if they're under the stairs?'

She's about to put the kettle onto the stove when she notices Andrew standing in the doorway watching her. 'Yes?' she asks.

'How was your night?'

'Okay, but I'm glad it's over. It's a mug's game.'

'You and Brian may have decided it's over, but I haven't been consulted, and neither has Linda.'

She puts the kettle onto the gas ring then looks at him and says, 'It takes four to play. Linda knew it was going to be the last time, and two of us have said we don't want to play again.' She lights a match and puts it to the gas; the small explosion makes her voice louder than she intended, when she says, 'So the game is over!' She turns to look at him, and softens her voice when she says, 'For Dylan's sake, we must make our marriage work. Sleeping with other people will only pull us further apart. I know I haven't been the best of wives. I'm sorry, but all that's changed. Things will be different from now on. Linda's been a wake-up call. I have to admit I was jealous when you went to her last night.' She walks towards him, rests her hand on his shoulder and smiles. 'The picnic can be the start of things to come; it'll be fun. We should spend more time together; perhaps it will help us get back to how it was when we first met.'

'Getting back to how it was is a tall order. I agree we should make an effort for Dylan's sake, but it won't stop me seeing Linda.'

Chapter 20

Brian pushes his plate away then stands up from the table. 'See you tomorrow,' he says as he picks up his keys and wallet.

'What time?' asks Linda.

He puts the wallet into the back pocket off his jeans. 'It could be late afternoon but expect me when you see me.'

She waits for him to leave the room, listens for the sound of the flat door closing behind him, then, with a sense of relief, she picks up his dirty plate. She scrapes the greasy crusts of bread and the squashed cigarette butt into the bin and closes the lid; if only it was as easy to dispose of Brian, she thinks.

She washes the dishes, walks into the sitting room, and gazes out of the window. Now that Brian has gone, and with time on her hands, she should try and catch up with some of the writing-group homework. She doubts if she will be able to concentrate though; the only thing she can think about is seeing Andrew. She has two and a half hours to kill before they meet, but the intoxicating feeling that pumps through her veins fills her with energy, makes her want to change her clothes into something cool and bright and go out into the sunshine.

Moving quickly, she leaves the sitting room, goes into the bedroom and opens her dressing table drawer. She puts her hand to the back of the drawer and pulls out a pair of lace-trimmed, black nylon panties. She had bought them with Andrew in mind – until now, as long as her underwear was clean, she hadn't worried about what she wore under her clothes; but, other than the peach coloured bra and pants set her mother gave her for Christmas, her underwear is not only plain, it is verging on tatty. She takes off the jeans and T-shirt she is wearing, removes her white cotton pants and puts on the new pair. The hem of the red cotton skirt she bought at the church jumble sale is now repaired and ironed; she takes it from the wardrobe and steps into it, chooses a white cheese-cloth blouse and pulls it over her head. She looks under the bed, sorts through a miscellaneous collection of footwear, pulls out a pair of brown, Cuban-heeled, peep-toed shoes, and slips them on. She goes to the mirror, puts a touch of lipstick to her lips and runs her fingers through her hair, then grabs her bag from the hook behind the hall door and leaves the flat. The feeling she gets when she pulls the door shut behind her is, metaphorically, like locking her troubles in a cupboard. Her feet hardly touch the stairs as she hurries down them. Mrs Jones is in the hallway sorting through the mail. Linda says a cheery hello. Before Mrs Jones has time to start a conversation, Linda is out of the house and onto the pavement.

Smiling at the prospect of the day in front of her, Linda strides down Regent Street, swinging her bag. She stops to admire the clothes in a boutique's window. From there, she wanders to the antique market, takes her time looking over trestle tables laden with bric-a-brac, pauses to pick up and examine a piece of pottery. When she leaves the antique market, she makes her way to Victoria Square. The square is busy with shoppers. A couple of children, similar in age to Ben, holler with laughter as they tear around on brightly coloured scooters. One of their mothers chases after them, shouts at them to be careful. Seeing the children makes Linda think about Ben and she wonders what activities Gloria has planned for the day. She catches the aroma of roasting coffee and looks towards a café. The door is open;

people are sat at shiny red tables enjoying the shade of the building. Linda walks over to the café, goes to the counter, and takes her coffee outside to sit and watch the world go by.

When she leaves the café, Linda heads for the lanes that lead to the docks. The cobbled paths, the stone walls, the scent of roses, are memories she will keep and cherish forever. Every detail is with her: the brush of Andrew's arm against hers, the sound of his breath as they climbed the steep paths; the anticipation, the excitement. Her nervousness returns as she hurries down towards the docks. Not in her wildest dreams would she have believed she would walk these lanes again to meet him, and that the circumstances would be so different.

She reaches the bottom of the hill; The Coronation Tap is only a few yards away. She's not sure of the time, but feels she is a good ten minutes early. Not wanting to sit in the pub on her own, she looks for an out of the way place where she can wait. She notices a shop opposite the pub and crosses over the road to see what is in the window. She looks at the display of hats, turns away to glance up and down the road; nobody is around, but she has a sudden fear that someone may drive past and recognise her. A bell rings as she opens the shop door. She goes inside, and a woman comes out of a back room. 'Can I help you?'

'I'm looking for a hat,' says Linda, while wishing she'd had the nerve to have gone straight into the pub.

'May I ask what occasion you need it for?'

Looking at the style of hats that are in the shop, Linda says, 'A wedding.'

'What colour outfit are you going to be wearing?'

Linda is about to point to a large brimmed, pink velvet creation when she spots Andrew going into the pub. She turns to the woman. 'I'm sorry. I've changed my mind. These days not everyone wears hats to weddings; I think I'll go without one. I'm sorry, but I have to go. I've an appointment.'

Without a second thought, she leaves the shop and dashes across the road. She steps into the pub, stops at the door to let her eyes adjust to the pub's dim interior. A few men are stood waiting at the bar; Andrew is amongst them. She walks towards him and touches his shoulder. He turns and smiles. 'Well timed; what can I get you?'

Not being used to ordering drinks at bars, but feeling a celebration is in order, she says, 'Wine, something cold and sweet.'

'Find a table,' he says. 'I'll bring it over.'

She chooses a quiet corner where she can sit with Andrew in view. The pale blue jacket he wears is becoming familiar; some might say it's old-fashioned, but his out-of-date clothes is one of the many things she likes about him. She watches him pay for the drinks. He casts his eye around the room looking for her; she waves, and he weaves his way towards her. He puts the drinks onto the table and pulls out a chair. 'Did you manage to get away without too many complications?' he asks as he sits opposite her.

'Brian didn't suspect a thing. He seems to be in a pretty good mood at the moment. I expect he's got another woman in tow. That's probably the reason why he hasn't mentioned wife-swapping again. I left the house soon after he did. I took my time getting here - did a bit of window shopping, looked around the antique market, treated myself to a coffee. Did you know there's a milliner across the road?' she asks. 'I was surprised. I can't imagine people around here buying those sorts of hats.'

'They used to do a roaring trade,' he says. 'I went there with Pattie once; she was buying a hat for a wedding. She said it had the best selection in town. All these small specialist shops are becoming things of the past. Milliners, umbrella repair shops, tailors, cheese shops. They'll all be gone; people prefer to do their shopping in one big building.'

Pattie's name causes her to ask, 'How is Pattie?'

'She's okay. I did tell her about us. She's not happy, but I don't feel guilty; she's had her fair share of lovers. She said she doesn't want you coming to the house. I don't know how that will affect Ben coming around to play. I will have to talk to her about Ben. Though, when it comes to you... You see, she never brought her lovers to the house.' He stops speaking for a brief moment then says, 'Well only once, but I knew who he was, and it was for a particular reason.' She doesn't ask, but Linda wonders what that reason could have been. Andrew continues telling her. 'We must think of some way the boys can get together; it worries me that what we do has an impact on their young lives. But I have got good news. I spoke to a colleague of mine, Nigel, who owns a flat not far from here. He uses the flat to take his girlfriend. Nigel had a fling with Pattie a few years ago so l thought he owed me a favour. I've got the key in my pocket.'

A prick of discontent blights Linda's day: not only might their relationship affect Ben and Dylan's friendship, but the bed they will be making love in is due to Pattie and is one she had used herself.

'You are pleased?' he asks.

'Why did you tell Pattie about us? What if she tells Brian?'

'I told you, Pattie and I don't keep secrets from each other; as for Brian, the last thing she wants is Brian coming to the house looking for me.' He takes her hand. 'Come on, everything's going to be alright, I promise. What about lunch? Let's have a bite to eat here then we'll look at the flat.'

The road the flat is in is not far from the pub. The buildings are small and neglected, the road littered with windblown rubbish. The flat is tiny: a kitchenette, with a few mugs, a kettle, and just enough room to make a cup of tea. The toilet looks as though it has been put in a cupboard; there is a basin, and a clean towel hangs behind the door. On a shelf is a tube of deodorant, a brush and comb, and a packet of Durex. There is one other room; it is sparsely furnished with nothing more than a wooden chair, a double bed, and a large gilt-framed mirror hanging on the wall. The floor is covered, wall to wall, with sea-grass matting.

'What more do we need?' laughs Andrew.

'What do we do with the sheets when we leave?' asks Linda.

'Nigel said strip the bed and put them on the floor. A woman calls in each morning to see what needs doing. I said I'd pay towards the cost.' He puts his arm around her and pulls her towards him. 'What's the matter? You're very quiet.'

'It feels strange. I don't like to think Pattie's been here; it's as if we're all tied up in this together, even Nigel.'

Andrew undoes the buttons on her blouse. 'The only thing Pattie knows is that I'm seeing you. She knows nothing about the key nor that I've spoken to Nigel. Nigel has no idea who you are, or even your name.' He pulls the blouse from off her shoulders, drops it onto the chair, then unfastens her skirt. The skirt falls to the floor; she steps out of it and kicks off her shoes. He unclips her bra. She takes it off, then, still wearing the panties she'd bought for the occasion, she lies on the bed. She watches him remove his clothes, opens her arms as he joins her.

Feeling contented and relaxed, Linda lies in Andrew's arms. Their love-making had been all she could have wanted it to be. He is a gentle lover and considerate, does all he can to give her as much pleasure as she does him. His concern has touched her. She knows there are plenty of women who like sex but had always thought sexual enjoyment was a man's prerogative, that men have the upper hand and their needs come first.

Andrew hasn't told her what time they are supposed to vacate the flat, and she is conscious that time is marching on. She strokes his cheek, saying, 'Do we have to go? Could we spend the night here? Brian's not back until tomorrow.' She moves her head from his shoulder, looks at him expectantly.

'I can't. there's a Dracula film on TV that Pattie wants to see. She doesn't want to be on her own, so I promised I'd watch it with her. It doesn't start till nine so we've plenty of time.' He kisses her cheek. 'There are lots of things I want to discover about you, like what do you have for breakfast, what books do you read, how often can we meet? When will I see you again?'

Pattie had been far from Linda's mind, but her name has started to take the shape of a spectre, appearing when she least expects it. Trying to keep the disappointment out of her voice, she says, 'I'm working tomorrow morning. Mum's expecting me to go straight from there to pick up Ben, though she won't mind me being late. If I let her, she'd be happy to have him the whole of the summer holiday. We can have a couple of hours together before I catch the bus. Tell me what your timetable is; I'll speak to mum and try and fix Ben's days with her to whatever your availability is.'

Chapter 21

It's been a difficult time for Pattie, and the school holiday has dragged on more than usual. It would have been worse if it hadn't been for Andrew being so supportive. He has watched Dylan when she's asked him to, has kept her company most evenings after Dylan has gone to bed, although she would have appreciated it even more if she didn't always have to ask for his help, if he would do some of the things she wanted automatically. She doesn't have to look far to know why Andrew is so distracted; it's clear to see there is someone and something else going on in his life. She would have to be blind not to recognise the signs, not to notice the days when he's taken more care over shaving, when he has remembered to comb his hair; the quick look in the mirror before he leaves the house.

They still argue - Andrew is unbendable when he wants to be. Most times Pattie will let him have his way, but when it comes to Linda bringing Ben to the house to play, Pattie will not budge; nor will she allow Andrew to take Dylan to Ben's house. Finding excuses when Dylan begs to see Ben gets harder by the day; all she can offer are lies and more lies. She hates to see Dylan upset, but what can she say? Not only does Pattie not want to speak to Linda, a premonition tells her to keep Andrew well away from Brian.

Sometimes Pattie hears Andrew quietly humming a tune; she catches him smiling, a secret smile that means he is thinking of Linda, that he is going over something she has said or they have done together: a joke, a walk in the countryside, a drink in a quiet pub. And it rankles to know it's her that has made him so contented. It is then that a wave of jealousy washes over her. It's then that she feels a trick has been played upon her. Andrew knew the unspoken rule in the game of wife-swapping: you swap for one reason only, that is sex; anything further can have serious consequences. But what can she say? She was the one to endorse an open marriage; it was her suggestion that he went to the playground and got to know Linda.

She has decided to hold her tongue, to let the affair run its course. She tells herself the relationship cannot last long: Andrew and Linda have nothing in common, no child to bind them, none of the joint experiences that keep a man and wife together.

In the meantime, she concentrates on being the perfect wife; the meals arrive punctually onto the table, the house is spotless, and she is attentive to Andrew's every need. She makes sure Andrew knows that she is the one who's trying to make a go of their marriage.

Being the sweet little woman at home certainly has benefits. In exchange for her good behaviour, Andrew has made every effort to please her. Getting him to sit down and watch TV had been impossible, but over the past weeks they've watched a few programmes together, even "Coronation Street", a series she knows he hates. A couple of times she's been able to drag him out of his office and into the car for a family outing. He has also encouraged her to take piano lessons - she'd been forced into having them as a child, but the more her parents nagged her to practise, the more she refused to play. In the end, she became rude and rebellious towards her piano teacher and the lessons stopped. When she told Andrew she regretted her behaviour and would love to be able to play music, he surprised her by buying a second-hand piano and offering to pay for a tutor.

It's not just learning to play the piano that makes the lesson so enjoyable. Practising scales and playing "She's

Coming Round the Mountain" and "The Saints Came Marching In" would wear a bit thin if the piano teacher was not so good-looking. From week one, she noticed Tony's eyes staring at her cleavage; he seemed more interested in her breasts than what her fingers were doing. During lesson two he suggested they try a duet together; that was when his motive became clear. He squeezed next to her on the piano stool; they sat hip to hip, thigh to thigh, his leg rubbing against hers, her fingers touching his as they searched for the keys. "Clair de Lune" reached heights she never knew existed; she didn't know the tune could be so thrilling.

It was almost five minutes after the lesson was due to end, when neither of them had moved from the stool, that Tony said, 'Well, I suppose we'd better make a move.'

Pattie looked at her watch and said, 'Gosh is that the time? It certainly flies when you're having fun.' She gathered her things together and he walked her to the door. Before he opened it, she reached up and kissed his cheek.

'Do you always kiss your piano teachers goodbye?' he asked.

'Only the good-looking ones.'

'I've another student arriving in about ten minutes; next time you come I'll make sure we've a bit of time to spare.'

It's not only Tony's good looks that attract her, she finds his youth irresistible. A young music graduate, giving piano lessons in his mother's house until he finds a proper job and a place of his own, is refreshing; she's had enough of married men. As far as she knows, Tony is single. Unlike Brian, he's intelligent; there's more to Tony's life than driving a lorry from one end of the country to the other, putting notches on his belt each time he screws a new woman.

Pattie's mind is on Andrew when she puts the finishing touches to the salad, adds the servers and puts the bowl onto the table. In many ways, she and Andrew are compatible: they don't often argue on what is right or wrong where Dylan is concerned; Andrew lets her have her way when it comes to choosing things for the home - soft furnishings, appliances she thinks might make her life easier, deciding to paint all the walls in the house magnolia; she does the shopping and plans what food they will eat. The only difficulty is their sex life - her libido is higher than his; she is a little more adventurous. It's a shame wife-swapping didn't work out the way she thought it would. She is hoping that when the holidays come to an end, and Andrew is back at work, he will have less time to see Linda. Hopefully, then his infatuation with her will come to an end. Being Andrew's cook, cleaner, child minder and companion with nothing in return is beginning to annoy her.

She casts her eye over the table; the orange cloth is perfect, with the brown Susie Cooper dinner-set. She takes off her apron, walks across the room and opens the door. 'Dinner's ready.'

Dylan appears in a flash. 'What are we having?'

'Quiche. Run up and tell your father; he may not have heard.'

'I'm here.' Andrew walks into the room. Pattie doesn't ask him where he's been all afternoon, or who he's been with.

Dylan looks at the table and pulls a face. 'You know I don't like salad.'

'Salad's good for you.' Pattie puts a slice of quiche onto his plate and pushes the bowl of salad towards him.

'It's too hot to cook,' she tells Andrew, 'so I went to the new delicatessen.'

She looks at Dylan. 'One lettuce leaf and a slice of tomato is not enough.' She takes the servers from him and puts a generous portion of salad onto his plate.

She turns back to Andrew. 'Do you like the quiche? It's great to have the delicatessen so nearby; they've a huge range of olives, black and green, and such a selection of cheeses. Dylan! Stop playing with your food. Don't look at me like that. You look tired; you'd better start having a few early nights before you go back to school.'

'And I'll be glad,' he says, smashing his quiche with his fork.

'Stop that. Eat your food properly.'

'Do as your mother says,' demands Andrew.

Dylan glowers at them. 'I want to see Ben. Why doesn't he come 'round anymore?'

'You'll see him in school on Monday.' Pattie tells him.

'I don't want to wait till Monday. I haven't seen him for ages. I want to see him today. I want him to come here.'

'How do you think he's going to get here? Don't keep on about it. Eat your food,' says Pattie.

'You could ask his mum; she'll bring him.'

'I said no! How am I to get in touch with her? She's not on the phone; they might not be in, and even if they are I don't have the time to walk all the way there and bring him back here.'

Dylan looks at Andrew. 'Dad?'

'Be quiet. Do as you're told.'

Dylan storming out of the room has left a silence as heavy as a thunder cloud. Pattie reaches across the table and scrapes the remains of their food onto Dylan's plate. 'This weather's enough to take away anyone's appetite,' she says. 'They say it won't last long. The forecast predicts rain by the end of the week.'

'About time,' replies Andrew. 'The country's looking more like the Arizona desert. I was talking to the woman next door; she told me she's started watering her garden with bath water.'

Pattie carries the dishes to the sink.

'Let me give you a hand with those,' says Andrew, standing up from the table. He waits beside the drainer with a tea towel in his hand, telling her, 'I went into town this afternoon; I've been trying to smarten up my wardrobe. I was beginning to look scruffier than my students.'

So that's where you were, thinks Pattie as she hands him a plate.

'I want to thank you, Pattie.' She turns and looks at him. 'I appreciate what you're doing. I know it's not what you want... Linda's filled a space in my life, and it's not just sexual... What I want you to know is, you and Dylan come first. I won't let you down. I don't want to lose either of you.'

Pattie feels no need to reply. His words seem to have lightened the room's atmosphere and they finish the dishes in a comfortable silence. When Andrew puts the tea towel on its hook to dry, he says, 'I need to sort my desk out. I won't be long. I'll join you later.'

Pattie pulls the plug from the sink and looks at him. 'While you do that, I'll see how Dylan is.'

Pattie hears Andrew leave his office, his foot on the stairs. She goes to the record-player, sets the turntable turning, puts the needle onto the record. John Williams' classical guitar piece "Cavatina" flows through the room. The music, the low light, the warm night air coming through the open window, the bottle of whiskey and two glasses waiting on the coffee table give the room a harmonious, intimate feel. She smiles at Andrew when he walks into the room and says, 'There's nothing much on TV, so I thought it would be nice to listen to music.'

She can't remember the last time she has sat so close to him. The whiskey has relaxed her, has given her a sense that all is well. They say very little as they listen to the music. They know the recordings well; the records are ones she and Andrew had chosen together. They take her back to a place she thought was lost and she begins to think the night will lead him to her room. Andrew leans back against the cushion; she puts her head on his shoulder.

He yawns, gently shifts her head from his shoulder, then turns to look at her, saying, 'I think I'll go on up to bed.'

'Me too,' she tells him. 'I could do with an early night.'

They turn off the lights and she follows him to the top of the stairs. He's about to go into his room when she puts her hand on his shoulder. 'Will you sleep with me?' she asks.

'I... I really don't think I...'

'Just for tonight. I'm not asking for sex... it's... it's just that sometimes I get so lonely.'

Like effigies in a cathedral, they lie side by side. Pattie turns towards him. Her hand touches his chest. If it wasn't for its rise and fall, she would question if he was there at all. She moves her hand to his waist. 'Andrew,' she whispers. 'Hold me.' He doesn't answer. She kisses his shoulder. Still he does not move. She turns away from him, stares up into the darkness, knowing very well who is on his mind. But why did he agree to come to her bed, she asks herself. And then, very gently, the covers move. She feigns sleep as he eases himself away from her side. He stands up from the bed, creeps across the room; quietly the door closes behind him.

Chapter 22

Since the new carpet has been laid in the attic rooms, Mr Roberts has been making more of an effort in keeping the place clean. Linda still has to remove dog hair from the bath plug-hole every so often; but other than coming into the flat for a bath, the dogs are kept in the shop - she guesses they must use the back yard to do their business. There are always mounds of dishes to wash, but Mr Roberts pays well; he's always pleasant and doesn't mind if she brings Ben – though, at the moment, from Sunday evening until Friday afternoon, Ben is with Linda's mother.

Linda is just about to finish her morning's work. On the draining-board there is one final mug waiting to be dried. She picks it up, rubs it with the tea-towel and puts it away; she gives the sink a final wipe, and hangs the damp cloth over the tap. Satisfied that the place is clean and tidy, she takes off her apron, checks to see if it will do another day, then hangs it on the back of the cupboard door. She rinses her hands under the tap, sniffs them to make sure the smell of bleach is well and truly gone, then goes to the bathroom. She combs her hair and re-applies her lipstick; when she's happy with her appearance, she leaves Mr Roberts' kitchen and goes down to the shop.

The dogs come out from behind the counter to greet her and she gives each of them a pat. Mr Roberts is on his knees sorting through a pile of magazines. She goes over to him. 'I'm off now,' she says.

He looks up. 'You're looking very attractive, Linda. Are you going anywhere nice?'

'Thank you. Only to mum's. Ben's back to school on Monday. I thought I might have to take him shopping. There's bound to be something he needs.'

He stands up, wipes the dust from his trousers and straightens his back. 'I bet you'll be glad to have him home,' he says as he takes a Crunchy bar from the counter. 'Give him this.'

She slips the Crunchy into her bag. 'Thanks; they're one of his favourites. I'll see you Monday.'

'Yes, see you then.'

She leaves the shop and looks down the road. Andrew is waiting for her, stood outside the tobacco shop as prearranged.

These past few weeks have given Linda a taste of freedom that she knows she will miss. Already she's wondering how to fit Andrew's timetable into her life, what with her cleaning jobs, taking and collecting Ben from school and pandering to Brian's needs. When the school term starts, something will have to go, she thinks. The only non-essential thing in her life is her writing course.

She walks towards Andrew, the excitement of meeting him marred only slightly by a wisp of anxiety. She keeps her face slightly turned away from the road, her eyes focused on the pavement; if someone was to see her meeting a man, if they were to report back to Brian, she daren't think what would happen. She steps into the tobacconist's doorway. Andrew joins her, takes her hand and kisses her cheek. 'How much time have you got?' he asks.

'Loads; Brian's working away tonight.'

'How do you fancy a day in the country?'

She opens her mouth in surprise; she had thought the afternoon would follow its usual pattern: a meal in a pub; the afternoon spent in Nigel's flat. The question is so unexpected she's not sure how to answer. 'How...When...Where?'

He points to the bus stop. 'Now; we'll catch a bus, there's one due any minute.'

'Of course, yes... I'd love to.' She feels a swell of happiness; this puts their relationship onto a different level. This proves it's not just sexual, that they enjoy other things, ordinary things, like going for a walk; they like being together.

The bus arrives, and they leave the shop doorway. Linda steps onto the bus. 'Have you been to Abbot Wood?' he asks as he climbs on after her. He pays for the tickets. 'There's a pub there that does really good food; the entrance to the wood is right next to it.' He follows her down the gangway. 'This might be the last chance for getting out and about; the weather's about to change.'

They settle into their seats. 'Have you thought, about buying a car?' she asks.

'No, why do you ask?'

'I just wondered.'

'I've thought about it but decided not to. They're a scourge. They used to be out of most people's pocket; now you can buy a second-hand one for as little as two hundred pounds. Soon everyone will want one. Before you know it, there'll be two or three cars to every family. The roads will be clogged, nobody will be going anywhere. There'll be overpasses, underpasses; houses will be pulled down to make way for roads. The countryside will be scarred with motorways; woods will be destroyed. Why do you ask? Would you like me to have one?'

'No, I only asked because it's usually the man in the family who owns and drives the car, and, as Pattie has one, I thought you might want one as well.'

'We're not what you'd call the average family. Pattie can do what she likes; she knows what I think about cars, but she has to make her own decision.'

‘I suspect Brian thinks he does enough driving,’ says Linda, ‘I can’t imagine him being interested in owning a car. As for me, I couldn’t afford a car if I wanted one.’

‘Are you still thinking about looking for another job?’ asks Andrew.

‘Not at the moment; what I do fits in with school hours.’

‘It won’t be long before the boys will be able to get themselves to school. In fact, Ben could call for Dylan on the way; they can go together.’

‘Ben has a busy road to cross; perhaps next year I’ll consider it.’

‘What about further education? You did say you might be interested.’

‘I am. I like writing, but that’s a bit ambitious. It isn’t going to give me a job. When it comes to training for work, I’m lost. I don’t know what I want to do.

‘Why not be ambitious? There’s nothing to stop you being a writer if that’s what you want. It’s not just about writing stories. Getting a qualification, a good command of English, can lead to many things: secretarial work, teaching, journalism. The local paper loves to know what’s going on; it can be anything from jumble sales to what’s on in the theatre. Someone will always want something written down on paper. Don’t let being a woman deter you from furthering your education; these days there’s almost as many women students as men. And from all walks of life; it’s not like it used to be: kids straight from private schools with rich daddies. I was a rarity, the son of a miner, with an accent to prove it, but it didn’t stop me. Don’t let anyone put you off; if you want to be a writer, write; you’ve a brain in your head: use it. Why don’t you let me help you? Let me read one of your essays. Bring it with you next time we meet.’

Linda doesn’t tell him she is planning to stop going to the writing group. That if she has to choose between the writing group and Andrew, it will be him. As for showing him one of her essays, it is out of the question. He lectures in English; she failed the Eleven Plus, and her work reads like a schoolgirl's. Being a miner's son only proves how clever he is. Anybody who lectures in a university has to be a bit of a genius. And his intellect is way above hers. She's never given roads, or the impact cars have on them, a moment's thought. She wants him to take an interest in what she does, but she's afraid he will be disappointed when he finds out how ignorant she is.

Andrew's voice cuts through her thoughts. 'Ours is the next stop.' She picks up her bag; a pang of guilt pricks her conscience when she sees the Crunchy tucked next to her purse.

They walk into the pub - being away from her locality gives Linda the confidence to put her arm through Andrew's. She stands close to him when they order the drinks. Together, they choose a table next to an open window, a table in full view of everyone who walks into the room. Their heads touch as they ponder over the menu. She watches him as he goes to the bar to order the food. Her eyes feast on him. She admires everything about him: the way he walks; the clothes he wears; his height; the shape of him. The food arrives. They take their eyes from each other to look at what is on their plates. She offers Andrew a slice of smoked salmon, opens her mouth to receive a prawn from his fork.

If they hadn't been so immersed in each other, one of them might have glanced out of the window and noticed the threatening sky. It isn't until they leave the pub that the drop in temperature hits their skin. They look up: as if by magic, the blue sky has been painted an ominous lead grey. 'What do you think?' asks Andrew. Linda slips her hand into his and they take the path into the wood.

A progression of people hurry towards them: teenagers wearing shorts and T-shirts; mums, dads, grandparents, children; dogs straining on leads.

'There's rain on the way.'

'A storm's coming.'

'I'd go back if I were you,' they shout.

'Thanks, we'll take a chance,' calls Andrew.

'Don't say you haven't been warned.'

Linda and Andrew carry on walking. The voices fade into the distance; soon the only sound is the crunch of their footsteps on the gravel path. Andrew stops and pulls her towards him. They kiss, and he reaches for the hem of her skirt.

She pushes his hand away. 'Someone might see.'

He looks up and down the path, cups his hands to his mouth and calls, 'Hello, is anyone there?' They listen. 'See, no one,' he says. He takes her hand and she follows him into the wood. He pushes aside the hanging ivy, snaps the protruding twigs, tramples the brambles to the ground as he leads her through the undergrowth. She lets him pull her along, not caring that her legs are scratched or where the journey might lead. There's a gust of moisture-loaded wind; a few heavy drops of rain start to fall, and they hurry deeper into the wood. They arrive at a clearing and a clap of thunder opens the sky. Gasping, laughing at the downpour, they run the last couple of yards to the large tree that dominates the space. She leans against the trunk. Andrew jumps and grabs a branch. Linda looks up, opens her arms, welcomes the shower of rain that washes over her. He puts his arm around her, undoes the buttons on her blouse, unclasps her bra, pulls down the zip on her skirt, and lets it fall to the ground. She kicks off her shoes; streamlets run around her feet.

She stands naked before him, waits as he undoes his belt, unbuttons the flies of his trousers. She puts her arms around him and he lifts her from the ground. She wraps her legs around him and he pushes himself into her. Sighing in unison, they move together. Rain runs with their kisses. Their passion, like the storm, electrifies the air. They climax, and she increases her grip, holds tightly to him, feeling the fragility of their love affair. Another crash of thunder makes her body jump. A strike of lightning illuminates his face; it is then she knows, without a doubt, that she loves him. She shivers. 'You're cold,' he tells her. He lets her down gently, reaches for her clothes. 'Let me help you.'

Other than a few men stood at the bar drinking pints, the pub is empty. The landlord gives the men a wink when he says, 'Beats me how anyone can get lost in four acres of wood crisscrossed with paths.' He looks at Linda. 'Before I call a taxi, I'm going to give that lass a whiskey; otherwise she'll shiver to death.' He presses the glass against the whiskey dispenser. Linda reaches into her bag for her purse; everything she touches is wet, soaked by the rain that has seeped through the flimsy material. Her purse will dry, but not Ben's Crunchy. She had completely forgotten about Ben's Crunchy!

Chapter 23

Pattie shoots Andrew an angry look. 'You should have known better. Lost in the woods; huh, do you think I was born yesterday?' Pattie's voice raises an octave or two when she says, 'I can guess what you were up to: looking for a secluded spot, I bet. Why else would you be there? Nobody in their right mind goes into a wood in the pouring rain. Anyway, you'd have to be some kind of idiot to get lost in them; it's not exactly Epping Forest. I'm surprised she agreed. I didn't know Miss Prim and Proper had it in her. I thought she kept her head down, didn't look further than whoever's floor she's scrubbing.' She hears the door open and turns around. 'Go out, Dylan; Daddy and I are talking.'

Dylan walks towards her. 'You're shouting. Who're you talking about?' He looks at Andrew. 'Why are you wet?'

Before Andrew has time to say anything, Pattie puts her hand on Dylan's arm, gestures towards the door, saying, 'Do as you're told. Go and watch TV or something. We'll have a chat later.'

Dylan shrugs her hand away. 'Don't worry, I'm going,' he says as he marches out of the room, slamming the door behind him.

She looks back at Andrew, is about to launch into another tirade of words, when she sees he is picking up his jacket; she strides over to him. 'Where are you going?' she demands.

'To my room.'

She lifts up her hand; the urge to hit him is overwhelming. 'I haven't finished talking to you,' she says, as she puts her hand down.

'You'll have to talk to me later. Right now, I want to get out of these clothes. When I've changed into something dry, I'll sort out what can go into the washing machine and bring them down. The rest I'll put on hangers and hope for the best.' Andrew makes a move towards the door and she steps in front of him. 'Perhaps you would rather I took them off here,' he says as he starts to undo his trouser belt.

Pattie steps away. 'No. Please. Go upstairs. There's a real chill in the air. You don't want to catch a cold before the new term starts.' He moves past her and she stares down at the floor. She listens to his step across the kitchen floor. The door opens; when it closes behind him, she lets out a sigh.

A weight of sadness has fallen on her. She realises it is all too late, that any chance of rekindling their relationship seems to have withered away. She goes towards the table wondering if he remembers the day they took Dylan to Abbot Wood. Dylan would have been not much older than two and a half at the time. Pushing the pushchair on the rough ground had been difficult and Andrew had to carry him. They had lunch in the pub. She wonders if he ate there with Linda. She sits down, asking herself what had been the state of their marriage on that day, whether it was already falling apart. The answer is probably yes; Dylan was a toddler when she felt she was becoming more and more discontented with Andrew.

Andrew is the same as he's always been. He hasn't changed, not one iota. He's still the reserved, impassive, indifferent to her feelings, person he has always been. Which is why her anger has not had the slightest effect on him, why it does nothing but bounce right back at her.

If only she knew how to rile him, if only she knew how to disturb that calm exterior, start a storm, release the passion that must be bubbling somewhere inside of him. If she could have raised it to the surface, perhaps their marriage would have stood a chance.

When she first met Andrew, she had found his persona - the unruffled, dignified academic - infatuating. She admits she was the one who did the pursuing, and it was partly because she saw him as an escape route to England. But it wasn't the only reason. She had found him attractive; she liked him a lot. When she discovered she was pregnant, she had been over the moon – luckily, she had kept Andrew's address, had written to him straight away, telling him he was going to be a father. She knew he would get back to her, that he would want to be with her and his child: he wasn't the sort of man who would shun his duty.

It was the joy in Andrew's face when he looked at his new-born son, the way he oh so tenderly held Dylan in his arms, that told her she loved him. When they took Dylan home to Andrew's bachelor flat, there was so much to look forward to; the future looked golden. They viewed dozens of houses and eventually bought the house they were now living in. Andrew was generous with his money, left the choice of décor entirely up to her, gave her the pleasure of choosing floor covering and furnishings, told her to plan the garden in whatever way she wanted.

The new baby became the pinnacle of her life and, what with the house to organise, she'd had hardly a minute to herself. She'd never complained that he'd left everything to her. She enjoyed looking after Dylan, organising deliveries, the decorators, the landscape gardener, the shopping, the cooking and everything else that kept the house running. She wouldn't have wanted it any other way; she liked being in control. But, at the time, she was tired; she didn't have the energy to worry that their sex life had become non-existent. It was when the house was to her liking and Dylan was sleeping through the night that she turned to Andrew for intimacy and companionship. It was then she discovered that her needs were greater than his; that the more she complained, the needier she became, the further he drifted away.

To Pattie's annoyance, her eyes are red from crying. She had thought the crying days were over, that although things were far from perfect she had managed to make her life sustainable - taking lovers dealt with that problem. And Andrew seemed to be happy enough, immersed in his work, content to let her have her way with the house and whoever and whatever she wanted to see or do.

Pattie realises she can't blame Linda for all of her troubles; Linda is as much of an innocent as she had been; Linda will discover soon enough that Andrew will back away if she gets too close. Though, innocent or not, Linda entering the scene certainly has changed the dynamics; she is the one causing the ever-widening gap between herself and Andrew; she is the one that has thrown everything into disarray. And what hurts, what hurts more than anything, is the time Andrew gives to Linda, time that could be spent with her and Dylan. The word jealousy stabs her thoughts; again, her eyes prick with tears. She wipes them away with the back of her hand, tells herself if it was casual sex she wouldn't mind, so long as it wasn't serious, nothing that might take him away from her. She had been hoping this fling with Linda would have blown over by now. She worries that the promises Andrew made about not leaving them will be forgotten. That if he carries on seeing Linda for much longer it will put their marriage in jeopardy. Despite Andrew being wet through when he walked into the house, Pattie noticed he was smiling; he had laughed when he told her how he and Linda had been caught in the storm. He looked young, carefree. And that is what she resents.

She hears Andrew's step on the stairs and she stands up from the table. She opens a cupboard door and pretends to sort through the jars and packets of food. When he comes into the room, she keeps her face hidden; the last thing she wants is for him to see she's been crying. He asks if she would like to talk to him and she shakes her head. He makes no further interjection and walks towards the washing machine; she listens to the sound of clothes being sorted, being pushed into the machine, the click of the lid, the chug of the motor, Andrew's footsteps across the floor, the door closing behind him.

She listens as he climbs the stairs, then sits back down at the table, drums her fingers on the table-top to the rhythm of her thoughts. If he thinks he's going to walk out of this house, if he thinks he's going to leave, he's got another think coming. The door opens; she turns her head away, thinking it might be Andrew. Dylan's voice makes her look round. 'What's wrong with everyone?' he says. 'Sometimes I want to run away.'

She stretches her arm towards him. 'Come here,' she says. He goes over to her and she puts her arm around him. 'Daddy and I would be very unhappy if you ran away. I'm sorry you're upset. Would you like to sit on my lap?' He nods and she lifts him to her knee. He rests his body against her. 'You're not too big for a cuddle either,' she says. She feels the shake of his head against her shoulder. 'Good; there's a real shortage of cuddles in this house.' She strokes his hair. 'Daddy got caught in the rain, which was very silly of him; adults do daft things sometimes. You mustn't worry about anything. Daddy and I love you very much; you mean everything to us. I promise, nobody, not you, not me, not daddy, are going to run away.' She kisses the top of his head, holds him close as she makes a vow to keep that promise.

Chapter 24

Linda looks at the calendar. A week late; she's never late.

One week quickly becomes two; three arrives almost overnight. Every time Linda goes to the bathroom she looks to see if she has started to bleed. When she gets up in the morning, before she goes to bed, she checks her underwear. Not a spot, not a drop of blood to ease her mind.

Even before the period was due she knew was pregnant. She can't explain it; it was a feeling, something in her inner core that made her aware of a quickening inside her. She'd had the same experience when she conceived Ben. She'd suspected weeks before the doctor confirmed it that she was pregnant. She hadn't expected Brian to be exactly pleased with her news, but she wasn't prepared for the steely look in his eyes, the anger in his voice when he said, 'Christ, what have you led me into?'

She slips her hand under the waistband of her skirt, touches her stomach as she asks herself, 'Who is the father?' It's a question that cannot be answered, though she knows it is far more likely to be Brian. Three, four, sometimes five times a week he demands what he calls his conjugal rights. The barbaric force he uses to enter her, the barrage of thrusts that beat with the force of a hammer, is nothing less than rape; but it isn't love that makes a child. Every time Brian finishes with her, as soon as he pulls away and lifts his body from hers, desperate to wash his semen from her skin, she goes to the bathroom - if someone is in the bathroom she makes do with the kitchen sink. But all her efforts to get rid of his semen - the used toilet paper in the toilet bowl, the scrap of damp rag thrown into the kitchen bin, the coil inside of her - did nothing to stop one tiny sperm making its way towards her ovary.

Before Andrew came into her life, Linda saw home and Brian as prison and jailer. The stolen moments with Andrew give a sense of freedom, have made her realise that escaping her captor will open her world. Because of her work, Andrew's timetable, and their domestic situations, the time that they can spend together is limited – they usually manage to meet once a week, occasionally, if they are lucky, twice. During the half-term and part of the Christmas holiday, Ben had stayed with Gloria. It was then that they were able to see each other a little more often.

Each minute with Andrew, whether sat in a pub having a drink, walking in the countryside, or wrapped in his arms in Nigel's flat, Linda has cherished. He tells her he loves her; she believes him. His words gave hope that a day will come when they don't have to say goodbye continually.

Now a shadow follows Linda's days, keeps her awake at night. She has made a decision: she cannot give birth to this baby; her life will be ruined if she has another child. The noose will tighten around her neck, put any thought of an escape from Brian even further out of reach. And what if he found out the baby might not be his? She could lose Ben; the law will be on Brian's side. She will be called the adulterer, not Brian. He will have every right to divorce her; he could apply for custody, and she cannot risk Ben being taken from her.

It is mid-January, almost two-thirty in the afternoon; the temperature is just below freezing. Linda and Andrew are in Nigel's flat; a grey light is coming through the window. They are in bed, lying naked beneath the blankets. Andrew is on his back; Linda is on her side, her leg is draped across his, her head resting on his chest. 'What is the matter?' asks Andrew. 'You've hardly said a word.'

She hears his question, but the words she has been dreading to tell him refuse to come, are held back by a lump, as hard as rock, inside her throat. She knows she must say something soon; time is ticking away. Soon she will have to get out of bed, get dressed and go to the school to collect Ben.

He puts his arm around her, pulls her up so her head is on his shoulder. 'Tell me what's worrying you,' he says.

She pushes herself away from him and sits up, bends her knees, wraps her arms around them, and pulls them towards her. 'I'm pregnant.'

For a moment he is silent; she hears him take a deep breath. He moves himself up into a sitting position. Their shoulders touch; she can feel his eyes looking at her, can picture the frown on his face, then he says, 'Are you sure? You might be wrong; have you seen a doctor?'

'I'm not wrong. I'm seeing the doctor tomorrow, but I know what he'll say; my period is never late.'

'I thought you had a coil. I thought it was safe.'

'So did I, but obviously it wasn't.'

'Why aren't you on the Pill?'

'I had a thrombosis after I gave birth to Ben; I was told the Pill would probably kill me.'

'What does Brian say?'

'I haven't told him. I'll tell him after I've seen the doctor.'

'What are you going to do? Will you...?'

'If you mean am I going to keep it, or am I going to have an abortion, what do you think I should do? Tell me. What do you think I should do? How do you feel about me killing a baby that might be yours? Though I doubt that it is; it's more likely to be Brian's. I don't want to have sex with Brian, I hate being in the same bed as him. Don't say I could refuse him; Brian doesn't listen to the word no. He sees me as his property. The law says it is a husband's right to have sex with his wife; what she wants or doesn't want is none of her business.'

If she hoped Andrew would come to her rescue, his silence tells her that is not to be. She can't blame him; who would want to share the responsibility of a child that may not be his?

'I'll probably have an abortion,' she says. 'I can't tell Brian this child's his when it might be yours. There is another reason I won't have this baby. I want to leave Brian. I don't love him; I hate him. I want him out of my life. If I have this baby, I'll never be able to escape. It's hard enough finding a place to live with one child; landlords don't want to know a single mother.'

A tear rolls down her cheek. If Brian was out of her life this child would be Andrew's. Even if they did not live together, she knows he would have supported her. She would now be preparing for this baby, looking for a home, looking forward to a peaceful future.

Chapter 25

Pattie opens her mouth ready to say something; then words fail her. She quickly gathers her senses together and in a loud angry voice exclaims, 'Pregnant! What? There's no need for any woman to get pregnant if she doesn't want to, not these days, not now the Pill's available. Before you start going on about me getting caught, that was different; no woman, or man, in Ireland could get their hands on a contraceptive, married or single. You knew what the situation was like over there; you're the one that had the opportunity to buy and bring a few packets of "Johnnies" with you.'

She stands glaring at him, waiting for an answer. He walks to the drinks cabinet, and she watches him take out the bottle of whiskey. He looks at her and asks, 'Do you want a drink?' She shakes her head; he takes the whiskey bottle and two glasses to the sofa, sits down and pours himself a large drink. 'Haven't you got anything else to say?' she asks. 'What is she going to do about it?

'I'll tell you what she's going to do about it, but first I'd like to say I don't think I've ever gone on about you getting pregnant; it takes two to make a baby. As for me not having any "Johnnies" on me, I was taking my mother to her home town for a trip down memory lane. I'd never gone any further than kissing a girl until I met you. Going back to Linda, she has a coil fitted. I presume she thought she was protected.'

'More fool her; anyone knows the coil's not a hundred per cent safe. Perhaps she wanted to get pregnant. Have you thought about that? Though I'm sure it's as likely to be

Brian's; he's bound to be taking what he considers to be his due; his sex-drive is like a steam-train with an open throttle.'

'You should know,' says Andrew. He takes a gulp of whiskey, cradles the glass in his hand, saying, 'Linda couldn't take the Pill for health reasons. She told me it could be Brian's, or mine. Though it wouldn't matter who the father is; Linda doesn't want a baby; she wants to have an abortion.'

With a sense of relief, Pattie sits on the sofa next to Andrew, telling him, 'I've changed my mind about that drink.' He picks up the glass, pours her a drink and hands it to her; she takes it saying, 'Thanks. I thought she looked pale when I saw her in the playground.'

'Oh, when was that? Did you speak to her?'

'A few days ago. No, of course I didn't speak to her. Dylan goes running after Ben as soon as he sees him, but I keep my distance.'

'Doesn't Dylan find it odd that you and Linda aren't speaking?'

'I don't think so; you know what kids are like, they're so pleased to see each other they don't give a second thought to what the grown-ups are doing.'

'Why do you have so much animosity towards her? After all, you were the one who wanted an open marriage. By the way, how's your sex life? Are you getting my money's worth with your piano teacher?'

'What do you mean your money's worth? If you're talking about my piano lessons, yes, they're coming along nicely. Anything else he gives me is free of charge.'

Andrew takes a deep breath before saying. 'I'm sorry, I shouldn't have mentioned Tony; you and he have nothing to do with what's going on in mine and Linda's lives. It's just... I'm worried about Linda. She's upset and I'm at a loss to know what to say. I don't suppose Brian will be much help.

Anyway, she's made up her mind. I didn't influence her one way or the other. It's her decision to have a termination. But what choice does she have? Foisting a child on Brian that may not be his, or telling him she doesn't know who the father is and ending up a homeless single mother with two young children. It's difficult for me to tell her what I think she should do. I agree the best thing is an abortion; but if I say that it looks as though I'm looking for an easy way out.' He takes a gulp from his glass, turns to Pattie, looks her straight in the eye when he says, 'Will you do me a favour and speak to her? She might find it easier to talk to a woman.'

Pattie twiddles with her glass; perhaps doing what Andrew asks will give them a platform to stand together. It will give her the opportunity to show Linda how united she and Andrew are. She will convey how much they depend on each other, that despite their differences their marriage is solid.

Chapter 26

Brian puts the cigarette between his lips and takes a drag. He continues staring at Linda as she stands in front of him; the only barrier between them, the small coffee-table holding a copy of the Daily Mirror and the cup of tea she had placed next to it. She is waiting for his reply, though whatever he says will not change her mind; nothing is going to dissuade her from what she is going to do. She watches the smoke curl from his mouth; she notices that the ash on his cigarette is ready to fall. He stretches his hand towards the chrome standard ashtray that is next to his armchair and flicks the ash in its direction. She watches the ash fall to the floor. She looks at his face, trying to read what he is thinking. He takes another drag, blows smoke towards the ceiling, then says, 'Well... having another one might not be a bad thing. Another kid means more child benefit. I know blokes who make a career out of having them; we could be raking it in. We might even get a council house, and...'

'I want an abortion.'

A look of surprise appears on his face. 'You what...?'

'I want an abortion. I don't want another child.'

''Why not?'

'I want to better my life. A child will get in the way. In a year or two Ben will be able to walk home from school on his own. I'll be able to start looking for a job.'

'You've got jobs.'

'I don't want to spend my life cleaning up after other people. I want a career. I want to study, to further my education.'

'You don't know what you do want: a job, or to further your education. Make up your mind.'

'I can have both. I can go to evening classes.'

'And who's going to baby-sit? Don't look at me; I've got enough to do. And as for furthering your education, what rot! Who do you think you are? You're a mother; that should be enough. Anyway, women like you don't do "further education"; if you'd had brains you wouldn't have failed the Eleven Plus. Be happy. A lot of women would love to be in your place: a husband, a healthy child, and a nice flat. What more do you want, Linda? What about Ben? He might want a brother.'

'What about you?' says Linda. 'You wouldn't be happy with another child. Think about it; you complain now about the noise Ben makes, and he's a good boy, well behaved compared to most. How will I manage? I can hardly make ends meet now. If I have a baby, I'll have to give up work. I can't expect Mrs Jones to look after a baby and Ben. And what about Mr Roberts and Mr Thomas? They wouldn't be very happy either, not with two children in tow. I'll lose my jobs as soon as they notice my bump. As for the council giving us a house, you must be joking: we've got two bedrooms; they'll expect the children to share.'

Brian leans back in the chair, stretches his legs out in front of him and rests his feet on the coffee table. He looks up at Linda. 'Do what you want,' he says. 'Be it on your own head. It's not my choice. I think it's morally wrong. It's as bad as murder. That's what it is: murder. I wash my hands of it; do what you like, my conscience is clear.'

Chapter 27

Pattie looks across the deserted playground to where Linda is standing. The last child has gone into school; the mothers have said their goodbyes and dispersed into their separate lives. The morning is grey. A drizzle of rain is beginning to wet the ground. Pattie's eyes are fixed on Linda's slender figure; she looks vulnerable on the darkening tarmac, a ready victim for the threatening sky. Pattie and Linda have not spoken to each other since mid-August; it is now almost February. Pattie can only guess that Linda would like it to stay that way, that Linda is waiting for her to leave the playground so she can go home. The school gate is the only exit. Pattie knows that Linda won't be able to stand where she is for much longer. She probably has work to go to; she will have to make a move soon. Slowly, Linda begins to walk across the playground. Pattie remains next to the gate. As she gets closer, Pattie can see how tired Linda is looking, how pale and drawn her face is. When Linda arrives at the gate, Pattie touches her arm. 'Linda...' she says. Linda pushes past her, walks through the gate, and out onto the pavement. Pattie follows her. 'Linda, I want to talk to you.' Linda keeps walking. Pattie hurries after her. 'Andrew told me you're pregnant,' she says when she reaches Linda's side. Keeping in step with her she adds, 'He said you're going to have an abortion. I want to know if there's anything I can do. It must have been such a hard decision, but the best one in the circumstances. Would Ben like to come and play? Dylan would love to have him around. He can come anytime. I'd really like to help. Perhaps, when you're in hospital, perhaps Ben can stay with us those nights; or when you come out:

you'll need to rest.' She puts her hand on Linda's arm, pulls her arm back a little to stop her walking so fast. 'Linda, please,' she begs. 'What good does it do, us not talking? The boys must notice. For their sakes, let's be friends.'

Linda pushes Pattie's arm away, looks at Pattie with hostile eyes, as she says, 'I don't need your support; my mother will have Ben.'

Linda's long legs stride down the pavement. Pattie chases after her. 'What does Brian think?' she asks.

Linda doesn't slow her pace or look at Pattie when she says, 'What do you mean? What Brian thinks is none of your business.'

'I mean, does he know? Does he know that you and Andrew are seeing each other?'

'No, he doesn't.'

'Good, he must never find out. I don't want Brian banging on our door. Andrew wouldn't stand a chance: he's no fighter.' Linda hurries on. Pattie struggles to keep up with her. 'It's a shame it all got out of hand,' she gasps. Swinging can be good fun. It's when someone gets emotional, that's when the trouble starts. It makes it all so complicated. If we'd enjoyed it for what it was, just a game, nobody would have got hurt. I know what I'm talking about: Andrew and I aren't new to it; we've wife-swapped before. There were never any problems; we played by the rules, no strings. Neither Andrew nor I would do anything to jeopardise our...'

Linda suddenly stops. She turns towards Pattie. 'SHUT UP!' she screams. 'I DON'T WANT TO HEAR ABOUT YOUR SORDID LITTLE GAMES, OR WHAT YOU AND ANDREW WOULD OR WOULD NOT DO. STAY AWAY FROM ME.'

Pattie had expected Linda to be upset; she had hoped she would be able to comfort her. She never envisaged such an explosion of anger, never thought she would see disgust in Linda's eyes. She watches Linda run down the street. Even when Linda turns the corner, when she disappears from sight, Pattie is still standing, staring, waiting, wanting to explain the reason why she lives the life she does, to make her understand that her need for Andrew is every bit as real and desperate as Linda's.

Chapter 28

The waiting room is stark. Other than a large clock with a loud tick, there is nothing on the green distempered walls: no posters, no pictures, nothing to tell you what is behind the doors marked 1 and 2. The only noticeable movement in the room is from a receptionist; she is standing behind a waist high desk, her face devoid of any expression as she flips through appointment cards. There are three lines of metal chairs in the room. Dispersed among the chairs sit a dozen or so women; every one of them has anxiety scratched upon her face. Despite the tick of the clock and a few hushed whispers, the silence in the room is so thick it could be cut with a knife. Most of the women hold their hands in their laps; some wring their hands together as though looking for warmth; others nervously pick at their fingernails. Every so often, a woman's eyes will drift to the clock, but mostly they stare at the floor, or gaze in front of them, blinded to anything but their own thoughts. There is no comfort in the room, no coffee-machine or pile of magazines; the only concession to anyone's needs is an overflowing ashtray on a red Formica-topped table. Gloria pats Linda's hand. 'You're doing the right thing,' she whispers. The receptionist calls Linda's name. Linda stands up and she is told to go into Room 2. 'I'm here if you want me,' says Gloria.

Linda gives a light knock then enters the room. A woman is sat behind a desk; she is engrossed in looking into an open black bound ledger lying in front of her. Assuming the woman is the social-worker assigned to her case, Linda stands waiting to be spoken to. Without looking up, the woman tells Linda to sit down. Linda places herself on the chair in front of the desk, fixes her eyes onto the social worker's grey fringe.

A minute ticks by before the woman takes her eyes from the ledger and looks up. She stares at Linda over the rim of her glasses, then says, 'How can I help you?'

The words tumble from Linda's lips. 'I want an abortion. I don't want this baby; I can't have it. The flat we live in is far too small. I'll have to give up my jobs; how can I work with a small baby? I need the money to supplement my husband's wage.'

The social worker's thin lips give a line of reproach. She continues to look at Linda as she lays her pen onto the desk. She takes off her glasses and places them next to the pen. Still with her eyes on Linda, she rests back into her chair.

Linda starts to perspire; her tightly grasped hands are damp, her body sweating inside her rayon jumper and nylon mac. She can feel the social-worker's eyes boring into her. Suddenly, unable to stop the words escaping, she blurts, 'I have, I mean I did have, a lover; it might be his. I can't pretend it's my husband's when it might not be. There's no other way; I must have an abortion.'

The social-worker's face is impenetrable. 'There was another way,' she says. 'No woman need get pregnant if she doesn't want to. Why didn't you go to your doctor and ask to be prescribed the contraceptive pill?'

'He wouldn't give it to me... for health reasons: I had a thrombosis after I had my son, which is why I have a coil; it let me down - you can ask my doctor. Please, I beg you, I must have an abortion. You must help me. I don't know what will happen if I have this baby. My marriage is not... is not a happy one. I can hardly cope now. A baby will...' Unable to put into words what a baby will mean for her, for her life, for her son, she stops speaking, lowers her head, too ashamed to say any more.

In a softer tone, the social-worker asks. 'What about this man, the man that might be the father of the baby? Will he take any responsibility?'

Still looking at her lap, Linda shakes her head. 'No, he's married.' She wipes away the tear with the back of her hand, then, taking a deep breath, she looks at the social-worker. 'I've decided not to see him again. I will let him know it is has to be over between us. I want my marriage to be over. If I have this baby, it will be impossible to leave. If I have an abortion, I promise I'll never get pregnant again. They can sterilize me; they can do it when they operate. Please, I don't know what I will do if you say no.'

The social worker picks up her pen. 'Alright. I'll recommend you have an abortion.' She rests her hand on the ledger's open page. Linda looks across the desk, watches the trail of ink, the flow of letters, the words that appear in the columns beneath her name. The social-worker stops writing. She looks at Linda. 'And sterilization. Is that right?'

Linda walks into the waiting room; her mother stands up and goes to meet her. 'What did she say?' she asks as they move towards the exit.

'I'm going to have an abortion.'

'You're doing the right thing, Linda. That flat's far too small for the three of you, let alone a baby. You and Brian should save a deposit for a nice house before you start thinking about another child.'

Chapter 29

Hurrying to get in from the rain, Pattie pushes open the door. Dylan pulls off his coat as he jostles past her. Pattie shelters in the open doorway, holds her umbrella outside and shakes it; puddles of water form on the floor as she brings it back inside. She puts the umbrella into the umbrella stand, closes the door, and almost trips over Dylan's red duffle coat which has been left on the floor. She picks up the coat, looks towards the stairs and shouts, 'Dylan, don't throw your coat on the floor, and where are your shoes? I told you to take them off. There'll be foot prints all over the carpet.' She hangs his coat on a hook, takes off her mackintosh and puts it next to Dylan's coat. She unzips her boots, pulls them off, slips on her slippers and goes into the kitchen. Surprised at seeing Andrew standing with the kettle in his hand, she exclaims, 'Andrew; you made me jump. I thought you said you were working all day and didn't want to be disturbed.'

'I thought I'd take a break. I was just about to make tea.'

'You look tired,' she says, taking the kettle from of him. 'Sit down; I'll make it.'

She fills the kettle, puts it on the hob, then joins Andrew at the table.

'Did you know Linda's in hospital?' she says. 'I've been talking to her mother; I guessed it was Linda's mother when Ben came out of school and ran over to her. Dylan was following after Ben, so I had a good excuse to go and speak to them. I asked her where Linda was, and she told me Linda went into hospital this morning. She said Linda had been having trouble with her tonsils and is having them taken out. Of course, I didn't let on that I knew the truth. She said the school has been very understanding, and that she was taking Ben home and keeping him with her until Linda is back on her feet. I asked how long she thought that would be and she said she didn't know. My guess is that Linda will be out in a few days; abortion's a very simple procedure. I asked if there was anything I could do. She said everything was fine and she was looking forward to having Ben. I wanted to give her my telephone number to let me know how Linda was doing but, of course, neither of us had a scrap of paper, or a pen. So I told her to give Linda my best wishes and we said goodbye, much to Dylan's dismay; he moaned all the way home about how much he is going to miss Ben, and why doesn't he come to our house anymore. I tried to explain but...'

The kettle's whistle cuts through Pattie's voice. She stands up, goes to the stove, and lowers the gas. Despite the concern and sympathy that Pattie has expressed. Despite the sound of laughter coming from a children's television programme in the lounge, the clatter of making tea, the clink of crockery being collected from the cupboard and the table being laid, Linda's name has cast a web of gloom, has filled the room with a depression that tells Pattie the conversation is about to take an ominous turn. She goes to the kitchen door and quietly closes it, picks up the tray of tea things and puts it onto the table. Not wanting to move on from the subject of Linda, but trying to lighten the tone, she chuckles and says, 'We'll have to make sure we steer clear of any such dramas in the future. I'm not talking about the pregnancy; no, that was just unfortunate, it can happen to any of us, and it's always the woman that has to bear the brunt. No, what I found worrying was her vulnerability, how needy she is. I'm sure Brian gives her a hard time, and I can't blame her for wanting to get away, but she's looking for a saviour, someone to rescue her from a rotten marriage, and that someone was you. The last thing I want to do is interfere in your life but, please, if you must have an affair, find someone who's stable, someone independent, someone who's not looking for a man to look after her and whatever offspring she brings. A man who'll...'

'WILL YOU SHUT UP.' Andrew suddenly stands up from the table; his chair falls with a clatter onto the floor behind him.

Pattie freezes, stands open mouthed with the teapot in her hand. She takes a step back, puts the teapot onto the work surface and turns off the kettle. It has shocked her to hear Andrew shout. Worried that Dylan might have heard, she whispers a reminder that he is in the next room.'

Andrew paces the length of the kitchen, turns around and walks towards her. He puts his face up close to hers and hisses, 'In answer to your question: no, I didn't know she was in hospital. I haven't seen her since the day she told me she was pregnant. The last time we spoke about Linda you accused her of getting pregnant purposely. I told you then that Linda does not want another child; she has other plans for her future; she thought the coil would protect her. And wasn't it your idea in the first place: yours and Brian's? The pair of you encouraged Linda and I to go to bed together.'

'I know, I know,' Pattie tells him. 'It was a big mistake, but lessons have been learnt. We must look to the future, try to make the best of what we have, for Dylan's sake. I like Linda. I hope that one day she'll be free of Brian and she'll find someone, someone who will be kind and supportive, someone who isn't married. I'm sure you want the same for her... don't you?' She waits for him to reply. 'Answer me.'

'What do you want me to say? Yes, I hope she finds this someone. Yes, I'll wipe my hands of her. I've had my fun and I'm not bothered what she does or who she does it with. If those are the words you want me to say, you're going to be very disappointed.'

‘What do you mean, disappointed? You’re not going to see her again are you?’

‘Yes, if she’ll let me.’

Pattie’s face distorts with rage. ‘Well, you’re a bloody fool,’ she hisses. Then, trying to keep her voice down, she says, ‘Where do you think it will lead? Being your mistress will never be enough for Linda. And what about Brian? Do you think he’ll stand by letting you fuck his wife? You’ve been lucky so far, but when he does discover it, he’ll beat the hell out of you.’ She takes a deep breath, ‘Come on Andrew; be sensible. You know what I say is true. If you must have someone, don’t let it be Linda.’

‘I don’t want someone.’

‘Have her then, but I tell you, if you ever, if you ever leave me to live with her, I’ll take Dylan away. I will. Believe me. I’ll take him to Ireland. If you want to keep your son, stay away from that woman.’

Chapter 30

Back towards the middle of September, a week or two into the autumn term, on a lovely clear day when the weather was crisp, and the leaves were crunchy beneath their feet, Andrew and Linda went for a walk in the university grounds. He showed her the department where he works, the room where he lectures, the refectory where the students eat their meals. He did not introduce her to anyone, but he had held her hand as though he was not afraid to show that she was his. She had felt proud standing next to him as students milled around them. It was another sign that told her she was not just a passing fancy, that he meant what he said when he told her he loved her.

It is now late February, but Linda clearly remembers that autumnal day; she also remembers the hours and days he works, the time he finishes, the exit he will leave by.

She has been waiting for him for a good ten minutes, standing partly hidden by a bush and a phone box, but with a clear view of the door that he will leave by. A few people have left the building and she is beginning to wonder if for some reason she has got the times wrong, or that he had taken the day off. And then the door opens, and he steps into the night. He is with an older man; they are deep in conversation. They walk down the steps together and stop to say a few more words. The older man laughs and Linda wonders if it is Nigel, if it is her they are talking about. They part company and Andrew walks her way. When he is a few feet away from where she is standing, she steps out from her hiding place. The light from the street lamp hits his face. First of all, he is startled; when he sees it is her, a smile transforms his face.

'Linda; you took me by surprise. I'm so glad to see you. I've wanted to go to the school, but Pattie has insisted on taking and collecting Dylan. I've been worried about you.' He moves towards her, is about to kiss her when she turns her head away.

'I want to talk to you,' she tells him. 'Can we go somewhere quiet?'

'Of course; the Bunch of Grapes is only a few minutes away.' He slips his arm through hers; she lets him lead her to the pub. The bar is heaving with students. 'There's a small snug at the back,' he says. 'It's usually empty; we'll go in there.'

He is right; there are just the two of them in the tiny room. She sits down, and he offers to buy her a drink. She shakes her head. He leaves her to go back to the busy bar they'd walked through. When he returns he is carrying a pint of beer and a glass of wine; he puts the wine in front of her.

He sips at his drink, listening intently to what she is saying. He doesn't interrupt when she tells him about her experience in the hospital, the lectures she had from nurses, the stories they told her of desperate women wanting babies, the shortage of babies for adoption now girls are opting for abortion. 'There were five women in the ward I was in,' says Linda. 'All of them had miscarried; all of them were grieving for the babies they had lost. I could see by the way they looked at me that they knew why I was there...'

She tells him about a recurring dream. 'I'm pushing a black pram, a big old fashioned one. The hood is so deep and dark it's like a cave. Somewhere, hidden amongst the black blankets, is a baby. The pavement is crowded; masses of people march towards me. I have to push and shove my way through them. Suddenly, I notice the pram has gone, disappeared into nowhere. I have a terrible fear that I've left my baby someplace and I can't remember where. I'm frantic;

I search through the crowd asking everyone, 'Where is my baby?' Linda stops talking. She waits for Andrew to respond to what she has said; his silence pushes her on. 'It says a lot, doesn't it, about how I feel? My baby is lost. Where is it now? Thrown away, burnt to nothing in a hospital incinerator. In the hospital there is a poster of a pregnant woman smoking a cigarette; written in red letters are the words "Smoking can kill your baby". The women who had suffered the miscarriages, the woman in the poster, the nurses, all of them were pointing a finger at me, telling me I am GUILTY.' She stops speaking, looks at him across the grubby table; his face is grim. He had been pleased to see her, had puffed up like a cooing pigeon when she told him she wanted to talk to him. Now the bounce will have certainly left his step.

His glass is almost empty. He picks it up and swallows the last dreg, points to her untouched glass of wine. 'Aren't you drinking?' She shakes her head. He reaches for her hand; she moves it away. 'I know it must have been hard for you,' he says. 'I wish I could have been there to support you, but you will get over it; it might take a while, but you will. You'll probably find this hard to believe, but I've been out of my mind with worry; I didn't even know you were in hospital until Pattie told me.' He tries to take her hand again; she moves it to her lap. 'What time do you have to be back?' he asks. 'We can find somewhere more private, somewhere where we can talk.'

'I've done all the talking I need to do. I must go home.'

'When will I see you again?'

Without replying, she stands up, hurries out of the snug, pushes her way through the crowded bar towards the door.

She doesn't look back, doesn't think about Andrew as she rushes through the streets. There is only one thing on her mind, and that is about to be dealt with. She enters the house, quickly climbs the stairs and lets herself into the flat. 'What time do you call this? You've been gone nearly two hours,' calls Brian. She goes into the sitting room; Brian is sat in the armchair with a newspaper in his hands. 'When you said you were doing some extra work for old man Thomas, I didn't think you'd be this long. Ben's still down with Mrs Jones. I expect she's fed him, but I'm starving. What is for tea?'

'I haven't thought about tea, I...'

'What do you mean, you haven't thought about tea? It's your job to think about it.'

'I want to talk to you. I have something to tell you.'

'Well it'd better be important.'

'It is. The baby... the baby I killed, it might not have been yours.'

'What are you talking about, not mine?'

'It might not have been yours.'

He looks at her open mouthed. 'Who's the fuck might it have been?'

'Andrew's.' The force of his hand across her face sends her flying across the room. The back of her legs hit the coffee table; she rolls across it and hits the floor. He grabs her hair, pulls her up and pushes her into the sofa; she can feel the spittle on her face as he shouts, 'You whore! You conniving bitch; you planned it, didn't you? The pair of you, you planned it all along. Stay there,' he tells her. 'I'm going to get Ben. He needs to know what sort of slut his mother is.'

She sits waiting, resigned to whatever fate is in front of her, not even caring anymore: the worst has been done, nothing can change it, and then she sees Ben. He is standing in front of her; behind him is Brian. His hands are holding Ben's shoulders, as though Ben is an offering, a sacrificial lamb, an atonement for her sin. 'Take a look at your mother,' Brian tells him. 'You need to know what kind of woman she is. A whore, a slag! Look at her, look at her; don't be taken in by that "butter wouldn't melt in her mouth" look.'

Linda's eyes meet Ben's; his solemn face, his not understanding makes her heart weep. Her inner voice cries, he doesn't know those words, doesn't know what they mean. She longs to hold him, to take him to a safe place where there are no harsh voices, no repulsive language, a place where only love matters.

'I think her mother needs to know, don't you Ben? I think Gloria needs to know what kind of slut her daughter is. Get your coat on Linda. Ben and I are going to walk you to the bus stop; you're going to tell your mother exactly what you've been up to. When you come back I'll be taking a little walk to lover boy's; he needs to be taught a lesson. Nobody fucks my woman without my say so, and I'll tell you this, you won't recognise him by the time I've finished with him.'

Linda's only feelings are for Ben. She yearns to hold his hand, but Brian has made sure Ben is under his control, on his side of the tiny platoon that march along the pavement. Her downcast eyes look across Brian to catch a glimpse of Ben's small figure; all she can see are the tips of his toes hurrying to keep up with them. They stop at the bus stop; Ben is holding Brian's hand. She wants to send him a smile, but he has not looked at her since they left the house. Brian stands silently staring at her, his eyes as hard and merciless as a Gestapo's. The bus arrives. Brian's parting words, 'If you're not back in two hours I'll come looking for you,' cause Linda's eyes to fall on Ben. Brian's words have made her realise how little he knows about a mother's love, and where her priority lies.

'Gosh Linda, why the face? You look terrible. Come in; you should have let me know you were coming. Where's Ben? What's happened? What is the matter?'

'I need to be quick, Mum. I haven't got long. I must get back to Ben.'

'You're shivering. I'll put the kettle on; you need a hot drink. Come into the kitchen. You can talk while I make it.'

She tells her mother everything. Things she had kept hidden from Gloria are now brought into the open: Brian's string of other women, his bullying, his violent attacks on her. She confesses that she has been having an affair with Andrew, owns up to the fact that Brian might not have been the father of her baby. She reveals the truth, tells Gloria the affair began with wife-swapping. 'I knew it was wrong,' she says, 'but I couldn't help it; right from the beginning I liked him, which is why I agreed to wife-swap. When Brian put a stop to it, Andrew and I carried on seeing each other and I fell in love with him. Getting pregnant brought the relationship to an end; the abortion threw me into a terrible depression. I don't know why I told Brian about Andrew. Maybe I want to see them suffer the way I have. Ben is the one I care about, he's the innocent one in all of this: poor, poor Ben. It was awful... if you could have seen his face... when Brian... Mum I can't bear thinking about it...'

Linda's admission releases her tears. She takes comfort from her mother's arms, allows herself to sob her pain. 'I have to get away from him, I have to,' she says.

'You should have told me,' says Gloria as she strokes the tear-wet hair from Linda's face. 'I could have helped you; there's a home for you here: for you and Ben, here with me. Go home, get Ben, pack a bag, and tell Brian you're leaving.'

Linda sits up, takes the handkerchief that Gloria offers and wipes her eyes. 'I will leave, Mum, but not now. Brian won't let me take Ben; I know he won't. Try not to worry.

When the time's right, when I can remove Ben safely without Brian getting his hands on him, I'll go; I promise. I'm more determined than ever to get away.'

Linda stands up, looks around the room for her coat. 'I must leave,' she says. 'Ben will be worried. Who knows what he might be thinking, and I don't want Brian dragging him out of the house to get me.'

Chapter 31

The urgent ring of the bell, the banging on the door, a man's thunderous roar, makes Pattie pick up the phone to call the police. Andrew's shriek, the crash of someone falling, makes her put it down and go running down the stairs to the lobby. Her heart is pounding when she sees Andrew lying curled into a tight ball on the tiled floor. For one moment she thinks he is dead, and then he groans and rolls onto his back. The front door is wide open. Guessing it was Brian that had paid a visit, she steps over Andrew, and closes the door, murmuring, 'Jesus, Andrew. What a fool you are.' She crouches down, puts her arm around him and helps him up into a sitting position.

She hears Dylan's voice. She stands up, steps over Andrew's legs, and goes into the hallway just in time to block Dylan's path.

His eyes are wide with panic. 'Mum, what happened? What was all the shouting? Why's dad...?'

Resting her hands on Dylan's shoulders, she says, 'Go back upstairs; Dad had a fall.'

Dylan tries to push his way past her, shouting, 'Dad got hit. I heard a man's voice. It sounded like...'

Pattie tightens her grip as she says. 'It wasn't anybody we know... it was a stranger... I don't know who it was... go back upstairs. I'll come and see you when I know Dad's okay.'

For a few seconds he struggles to get past her, then she takes his elbow and steers him to the stairs; reluctantly and still complaining, he climbs them.

She watches him; when he disappears into his room, she goes back into the lobby. Andrew is trying to push himself up from the floor. She helps him to his feet; ignoring his protest, she takes his arm and leads him from the lobby to the sitting room. 'Take a look at yourself,' she says as they walk towards the large antique mirror that hangs above the fireplace. She stands at his side as he examines his face. His left eye is no more than a red dot inside a swollen lid, his cheek slowly developing to the colour of a ripening blackberry.

Pattie's eyes leave Andrew's battered face and she stares at her own reflection. Sleepless nights have taken their toll, have dragged the life out of her, left her looking dull and tired, etched a cross-stich of anxiety around her mouth. Her nerves are stretched so tight they are ready to break. Even her hair has been neglected; the bleached end reminders of last summer are as dry and forgotten as a stick of seaside rock. 'I knew this would happen,' she says.

Andrew turns away from the mirror and looks at her.

'I knew Brian would find out,' she tells him. 'I hope you realise how dangerous he is. Brian knows a lot of people around here; he's well known in the pubs and betting shops. One of his cronies must have seen you together. Or maybe it was someone from the school, someone we know! Think, Andrew, think who it might be.' He shakes his head and she says, 'What will your students think? What will it do to your reputation? When I heard the bell and the banging on the door, I guessed something awful was about to happen. I was so frightened. It was bound to be Brian. I begged you not to answer; why didn't you listen to me? When you left I was so petrified I picked up the phone to call the police. When I heard your shout, I put it down and ran to you. I knew it would lead to this, that you'd be the one to get hurt. You wouldn't have a hope in hell against Brian. I tried to stop Dylan from seeing you, but how could I. And he knows it was Brian. I'm sure he recognised his voice, but what was I to say? That his best friend's dad punched his dad? I had to tell him something, so I lied. I said the first thing that came into my head, that it was a stranger; it was all I could think off. What will that do to him? He may never want to answer a door again! I'm not surprised this has happened; Brian would have found out in the end. With any luck this will be the finish of it, though, knowing Brian, he may not be off the boil yet.' Pattie opens her arms in despair. 'I hope you've learned your lesson,' she says. 'I hope you realise how important it is to stop seeing her.'

Andrew moves towards her, puts his arm around her, and pulls her to him; she rests her forehead on his shoulder. 'Sit down,' he tells her.

She shakes her head. 'I can't, I must go to Dylan; he'll be frightened. I told him I'd see him when I knew you were alright. It's late; it's time he went to sleep. That's if he's able to sleep.'

'You stay here; it'll be better if I go. He'll see me up and walking around. I'll tell him it's just a bruise, a minor injury, that my face will be back to its normal handsome self in next to no time.'

She gives a languid smile as he walks her to the sofa. 'Stay here,' he says as he plumps up a cushion. 'I'll get you a drink.' She sits down, watches him go to the drinks cabinet. He takes out the whiskey and a glass, pours out a large measure and gives it to her, saying, 'Don't worry; I'll make sure he's alright. As soon as he settles I'll be down.'

The silent room engulfs her. She is conscious of the strong taste of whiskey, the continual recall of events that have led to her sitting on the sofa. For the umpteenth time, she is back in the lobby, Andrew is on the floor... Suddenly the replay is interrupted; Andrew's voice is telling her, 'He's asleep now. Though he was very worried; he insisted we tell the police. I had to lie and say we would. I told him I'll do it tomorrow when he's in school. Though, if he and Ben get their heads together the truth may emerge. I started reading a story from a Rupert Annual; he was asleep before I got to the end, so I've turned out the light and left the door ajar so we can hear him.'

He perches beside her; she is still cradling the empty glass in her hands. He takes it from her, places it onto the floor. He sits back into the sofa and she leans against him. 'Maybe now we can concentrate on giving Dylan a stable family home,' she says. Closing her eyes, she rests her head on his shoulder. 'Perhaps I'll start sleeping better. I feel so tired...'

'I'm sorry,' he tells her. 'If I could have foreseen the chaos it caused I'd have stayed away from her... Though... I'm going to miss her... How can I explain it... she made me feel good about myself... the days seemed brighter. She made me feel... I can think of no other word than happy. It wasn't all down to sex, though it was a big part of it. I didn't realise how frustrated I was until Linda... I can see how selfish I've been. I hardly gave a thought to you and Dylan. I lost touch of what was going on around me. I departmentalised, put Linda in one box, you and Dylan in another and expected everything to be okay. Poor Dylan; what on earth must he have thought when he saw me on the floor? As you say, what is that going to do to him? Ben as well. I bet he's wondering why he doesn't get invited here anymore.' Gingerly he touches his cheek. 'And this: how am I going to explain it? You're right; I should have thought about what the consequences might be. I promise you, Pattie, I'll make it up to you, to both of you, you and Dylan.'

A sense of relief washes over Pattie; she lifts her head from his shoulder and she turns to look at him. 'Hearing those words takes a load off my mind,' she says. 'I don't blame Linda; if I'd been in her situation I'd be looking for someone like you. It was partly my fault. I should never have suggested swapping with a couple like them. Wife-swapping needs to be played with people of a similar class and mind, people who aren't looking to escape from the miserable lives they've put themselves in. At least Linda has a mother to help her. I really envied Linda when I met her mam in the playground. I know I moan about my parents, and I know how awful they are about you. I quite understand why you won't visit them. As I've tried to explain, the Irish are as racist as the English, even more so when their only daughter marries an atheist, but sometimes I'd give anything to see them.'

'Why don't you? When was the last time you visited them - three, four years ago? I'll look after Dylan. You'll be able to catch up with old friends. Take a bit of time to yourself.'

She hesitates for a moment before saying, 'Maybe... but... I don't know. I really need a break, a bit of time to myself... they'll wonder why Dylan isn't with me. And what about you? How can you look after Dylan? What about work? How will you manage?'

'We'll be fine. When you and Carol went to London I managed well enough. Dylan didn't complain about the food and the house was reasonably tidy when you got back. As for your parents, it'll be far easier without Dylan. They might not go on about getting him christened and such. You'll be able to meet up with friends. The weather won't be so good this time of year, but there'll be waterproofs in the house and you love walking along the coast. Don't worry about Dylan, or work; it won't be a problem. I can drop him off at school on my way to the university. If I get stuck later in the day I'm sure Carol will pick him up.'

Pattie begins to warm to the thought. Giving Andrew another taste of organising childcare and looking after the house will be good for him. The kitchen was in a bit of a mess when she got back from London, but she thought he did start to appreciate her a little more. Then there's her piano lesson; the extra time Tony allotted for other things has dwindled to not much more than ten minutes. She suspects he has a girlfriend; not turning up to a few lessons might revive his interest. And as for Mam and Dad; being able to get out and about without having to beg them to babysit will certainly make life easier. 'Perhaps you're right,' she says. 'A walk by the sea, having a drink with old friends is just what I need.' Suddenly a picture of Linda's lonely figure standing in the playground causes a shadow to fall. She avoids Linda as much as she can. She wonders if Andrew will be able to do the same. She looks Andrew in the eye and says, 'Are you sure you'll be... Linda will be in the playground.'

'I can't stop her being there. You'll have to trust me.'

She looks at his face, thinking hopefully the beating he received from Brian has given more than a bruise. Andrew's no macho; she's pretty sure he won't want a repeat of what happened today. The thought of losing Dylan will make him think twice before having anything to do with Linda. He believes what I say. He knows that if I get one sniff of a suspicion that he and Linda are together, I will carry out my threat and take Dylan away.

'Of course,' she says. 'Of course I trust you. I'll give Mam a ring and tell them I'm coming. If they say anything about Dylan not being with me, I'll tell them they'll have to get over the silly nonsense about not getting in an airplane because it might crash, a ferry because it might sink, and come and stay with us.'

Chapter 32

When Brian told Linda he had given Andrew the thrashing he deserved, she'd felt nothing. It was as though all reaction was buried in a pit. The only conclusion she came to as to why she had been so inert was because she had been in a state of shock. It took time to recover from the numbness that engulfed her but when it left a veil lifted and it became clear she needed to take control of her life.

She told herself that the first thing she must do was to speak to Andrew. She found herself consumed in a quest to find him. She searched for him at every opportunity. Praying that Pattie would not catch sight of her, she made numerous trips just to walk past their house, to gaze up at the windows in the hope that he might see her. She made detours, traced the steps she knew he took, planned her route, turned each corner, trusting fate to send him to her.

One evening, a sudden impulse made her tell Brian that Mr Thomas wanted her to work a few extra hours. Brian believed her; in next to no time she had grabbed her coat and left. She knew if she hurried she would catch Andrew leaving the university. When she arrived at the campus, she noticed straight away it was deserted. There were no students milling around the main entrance, and the large imposing door was shut. The temperature had dropped; sleet was starting to fall. She was planning her next move when the door opened and a man in a boiler-suit stepped outside. She went over to him. 'They went home hours ago,' he told her. 'The boiler packed in; it might be ready tomorrow, but I doubt it.'

Ignoring the inner voice telling her she was wasting her time, Linda ran to his house. A light shone through the curtains of an upstairs window. She convinced herself the room was his: hadn't he told her his office was on the first floor, that he and Pattie slept in separate rooms? She thought if she wished hard enough she could send him a message, that he would pull back the curtain, see her standing outside, leave the house and join her. The curtain didn't open. In the end, it was the shivers that ran through her body, the weight of her wet coat, the thought that Brian might come looking for her, that forced her home.

Disappointment didn't mean giving up looking for him; she still went out of her way in the hope their paths would cross. There was one exception; one route to be avoided. Walking next to Pattie on the journey to and from school would be deplorable; she was sure Pattie would feel the same. It was bad enough seeing each other in the playground: actively ignoring each other; avoiding eye contact; standing apart, while the boys, as pleased as ever to see each other, happily chatted and played, chased each other into school, not noticing the frozen lake that had spread itself between their mothers.

She knew she would see Andrew somewhere, someday, but it still comes as a surprise when she walks into the playground with Ben and sees him and Dylan stood amongst the women and children crowding in front of the school door. Ben's face brightens when he sees Dylan and he calls his name. Andrew turns, and his eyes meet Linda's. She can feel Andrew watching her as she follows Ben across the playground. It must be all of two weeks since Brian hit him. She thought any injuries would have faded by now, but as she gets closer she can see the bruise, the sunshine-yellow stain on Andrew's cheek. The school bell rings. She kisses Ben, waves goodbye, and watches Ben and Dylan go into school. She is conscious that Andrew is standing next to her. She turns towards him. The bruise is more extensive than she had envisaged. 'I'm sorry you were hurt,' she says.

He gives a slow smile, touches the bruise on his face. 'It's no matter. It did wonders for my reputation; I've become the talk of the university.'

She begins to relax. 'What have they been saying?'

'That I've been playing around with someone else's wife and her husband gave me a beating.

She chuckles. 'News travels fast.' They walk towards the school gate. 'Where is Pattie? Why are you taking Dylan to school?' she asks.

'Pattie's in Ireland visiting her parents.' He looks around. 'We must be careful. I promised Pattie I'd stay away from you. Carol might still be here; Pattie's bound to have asked her to keep an eye on me. I don't want to sound paranoid, but there are others who might be watching. Somebody told Brian about us: we don't know who that was.'

'I need to talk to you,' she says. 'It's important; somewhere we can be alone; this morning if possible.'

He hesitates; for a moment she thinks he is going to refuse, then he says. 'Alright, come to the house. We won't walk together; we'll part here. Come through the back way. I'll leave the door open.'

The moment she enters the house she feels something is wrong. She understands why he had been nervous in the playground, but now they are on their own, she had expected, at least, a peck on the cheek. She follows him into the kitchen. He doesn't ask her to sit down, doesn't say anything as he makes and pours the coffee. She takes the steaming mug from him; he takes his coffee over to the window, where he stands watching her. 'What is it you want to say?' he asks.

She wonders why his behaviour has changed towards her. Did it make him uncomfortable hearing about her experiences in the hospital and the description of her dream? Or was it the way she suddenly got up and walked out of the pub? She will explain to him that the abortion had had a profound effect on her, will try and make him understand that she was depressed, grieving for the loss of her baby. But first she must confess. She steels herself for what she is about to say. Aware that it could destroy their relationship, she almost changes her mind. Then she tells herself, if they are to go into the future together, she must have a clear conscience. She puts the coffee onto the table, picks it up and takes a sip, puts it down, straightens her shoulders and looks across the room at him. 'It was me,' she says. 'I told Brian. I told him the baby might be yours.'

'Sorry,' he says. 'What do you mean?'

'Nobody has been spying on us; it was me. I told Brian.'

'You told him! Why? You must have known what the outcome would be.'

'I've asked myself that question. I think maybe it was because I was angry, angry with you and Brian. Angry because I had to make a terrible decision while you and Brian were able to get on with your lives, could go into the future without the tower of guilt that I carry. Perhaps I wanted to punish you. Telling Brian dealt with you both in one blow. I hurt his pride and he hurt you.'

Andrew walks towards her, stops at the table and pulls out two chairs. Linda sits down, and he sits beside her. He takes her hand, saying, 'I understand why you're upset, but I can't see how Brian, or I, could have made that decision for you.'

'The baby might have been yours,' she says. 'You told me you loved me. If that was true, you would have accepted the baby and loved it, whoever its father might be.'

She could tell Andrew so much more: how those fateful words not only affected her world, but Ben's as well; that Brian's bullying and demand for sex is nothing compared to the indoctrination he is forcing on Ben, how powerless she is to stop him trying to convert Ben into believing that women are sluts that can't be trusted. Whenever Brian has the opportunity, he tells Ben he must stop being a Mummy's boy, that he must grow up, that if he finds his teddy he will throw it away. She could say how her heart breaks each time she sees Ben sucking his thumb, hiding his teddy when Brian walks into the flat. She keeps these things to herself; sympathy is not what she is looking for.

'What is done is done,' she says. 'No one can bring my baby back. That problem has gone forever. I can never get pregnant again. What I do know is that I love you. I want to walk down a street with you without shame, without the fear that someone might see us. I want to be with you.' She waits for him to say something... 'Do you love me?' she asks.

She wonders if he is going to reply and then he nods his head, 'Yes.'

'Will you leave Pattie?'

'That's a hard one; there's Dylan to consider.'

'Do you love Pattie?'

'Not in the way I love you, but she's my wife; I have an obligation to provide and look after her.'

'So you should, but you don't need to live together; you've told me you lead separate lives, so why not have separate houses? They can live nearby; you can see Dylan as often as you want. You say you love me; if you mean it you'll want to be with me. Will you leave Pattie so that you and I can live together? Or is it Brian you're worried about?'

He takes her hand. 'I'm not worried about Brian; he'd soon get tired of chasing after me. I mean what I say; my feelings haven't changed. But I've made a promise to Pattie. I have told her I'll have nothing more to do with you; seeing you, being with you now, has made me realise how difficult that is.'

He leans towards her, goes to kiss her. She moves her head away, saying, 'Will you tell Pattie you're leaving her to live with me?'

He shakes his head. 'I can't. Pattie told me she'll move back to Ireland and take Dylan with her if you and I live together. I can't let that happen. How often will I see him? A few weeks during the school holidays if I'm lucky. I'll miss huge chunks of his life. I can't lose my son; I can't replace my son with yours. I'll never be able to love Ben the way I love Dylan. You'd do the same; I know you would. But it doesn't mean we have to stop seeing each other. I'll rent a flat. It will be yours and Ben's, we can...'

His words fade to nothing as she stands up from the table. When she opens the door, his protests, the sound of his chair scraping against the floor, are tissue paper in the wind.

Chapter 33

'I knew it; I knew it. I had been a bloody fool to believe him,' thinks Pattie as she strides across the playground. Determined to get home before Andrew leaves for work, intent on ruining his day as much as his actions have ruined hers, she hurries out of the school-grounds. Ignoring the angry beeps from cars, she runs across the road: there is only one thing on her mind, and Andrew is going to know about it. She can barely catch her breath when she reaches the house. She pushes open the garden gate, dashes up the path. Carol's words are still thumping in her ears when she turns the key in the latch. She steps into the lobby; her eyes light with triumph when she sees Andrew with his coat buttoned and his briefcase in his hand. 'You got back quick,' he says as he makes his way to the door.

'I want a word with you,' she tells him.

He stops and looks at her. 'Can't it wait?'

'No, it can't. You'd better put that case down; what I have to say might take a while.'

'You can tell me later,' he says as he steps past her.

She grabs his arm. 'I'm going to tell you now; if you don't listen you'll regret it.'

He pulls his arm away, turns around, retraces his steps and puts his briefcase onto the hall table. 'Well,' he says, 'it'd better not take long; I've a class of students waiting to see me.' He follows her into the kitchen. 'What is it?'

'Carol saw you talking to Linda; you walked across the playground with her.'

''Is that it? You've stopped me leaving to tell me that? So what if I did talk to her? What if we did walk across the playground? Our boys go to the same school.'

'The boys had already gone into school! Carol said the conversation looked quite intense. I thought you were going to avoid her: that's what you said, and I was foolish enough to believe you. Is that why you encouraged me to go away? Was that the plan? Get rid of me and go to her as soon as I was out of the country? I wish I could make you understand that what you're doing is dangerous. If Brian gets wind of it, he'll give you more than a beating, I'm telling you. I won't stay here and subject Dylan to another round of terror. It was no idle threat when I told you I'd take him away. I will, Andrew. I'll...'

'I thought that threat was if I left you for Linda. I didn't know it included talking to her, or even walking next to her. What was I to do? Ben ran over to see Dylan, and she followed. I could hardly ignore her.'

'I always manage to.'

'Shut up. Listen to what I'm going to tell you. We did walk across the school grounds together, that's what people do. I would have told you about it, but I know how sensitive you are on the subject. Anyway, now you know half of the story, you might as well have the rest. If Carol was as vigilant as you were hoping, she'd have seen that when we left the school we went our separate ways, though parting company was a ploy.' He starts to undo the buttons on his coat. 'I must go and ring work,' he says. 'They'll wonder where I am. I'll carry on with this confession in a minute.'

Pattie pulls her poncho from over her head, throws it towards a chair and lets it slides to the floor. She sits at the table and nervously runs her fingers through her hair. She can guess what his confession will be; as Linda is involved, it can mean only one thing – he and Linda are going to resume their relationship. When she told Andrew she would take Dylan to live in Ireland, she never planned to actually do it. She said it to make him realise what was at stake, that the break-up of any family leads to painful decisions that will affect them all, especially the children. Just looking at the Irish landscape from the aeroplane window, seeing the wilderness of space, the empty miles, was enough to tell her leaving England is out of the question. When they circled Shannon Airport and a few isolated farms came into view, when her father picked her up from the airport and they drove past hovels that called themselves small-holdings, clusters of deserted ruins that spoke of hardship and poverty, she knew without a doubt that was not where she belonged. Growing up in the big house overlooking the sea, being the privileged youngest child of the vet and his wife, had been a childhood that most would envy, but she wouldn't want it for Dylan. The beaches, the moors were her playground; what she lacked was playmates. The house was four miles from the village; the only time she mixed with local children was during school hours. There is a big age gap between her and her three brothers; by the time she was ten years old, all three had moved away from home: Cormac to New York; Peter to Milwaukee; John was now living in Sydney. The obligatory Christmas cards are the only contact she has with them.

When Andrew comes into the kitchen, she sits up straight and turns to look at him. The buttons are now undone, but he is still wearing his coat; it sends a signal that says, as soon as he reveals his and Linda's plan for the future, he will go to her. She pulls her shoulders back. 'You were saying,' she says.

He sits opposite her. 'Yes, I was saying... Linda told me she wanted to talk to me; she said she wanted to go somewhere private. I thought Carol might be watching. I guessed she'd report anything she saw back to you, so I told Linda to make her own way to the house, that I would see her here.'

'What! You invited her here! Are you mad? I can't believe you were stupid enough to have her in the house.' She points her finger at him. 'There are a lot of people out there talking and gossiping. Someone will have seen you. Before you know it, Brian will find out and he'll be hammering on the door.'

'It was Linda who told him. She told him the baby might have been mine.'

Pattie looks at him open mouthed. 'Why? Why did she do such a thing?'

'I asked her that. She said it might have been to punish us, both of us, me and Brian. She said the abortion had left her weighed down with guilt, that she felt Brian and I got off scot-free.'

'Why did she wait till now to tell you?'

'I suppose it's because she hadn't seen me, which goes to prove I've been keeping out of her way. Seeing me in the playground gave her the opportunity to tell me. Why I'm telling you this is to reassure you that, other than Carol, nobody is spying on me.'

'So, is this the first time you've seen her since the abortion?'

'No, I saw her about a month ago. She was outside waiting for me when I left work. She was upset; she wanted to talk to me.'

'What about?'

'The abortion, how she felt about it.'

'So, when she came here, other than giving you the news that she'd told Brian you might be the father, did she say anything else? Was there any other ground-breaking news she wanted to tell you?'

'She wanted to know if I loved her.'

'If you loved her? What was your answer?'

'Yes. I told her I do love her. I also told her I had an obligation towards you and Dylan, that I cared about you. I said you had told me you would take Dylan to live in Ireland if she and I live together. I explained to her the last thing I want is to lose my son. I asked her if she and I could carry on seeing each other. I told her I would find her a home. But she refused. She walked away, out of this house. She didn't want to be my mistress; she wanted more than that, more than I was prepared to give.'

'So, you chose Dylan and I?'

'Yes.'

'Will you promise not to get in touch with her again?'

'I do; she is out of my life.'

'Are you sorry to lose her?'

'Yes, I am, but I had to make a choice. I want to be with my son. I don't want to be a distant father. I don't want to see him three or four times a year. It's the times in between that are important: school concerts, helping him with his homework, watching him grow.'

'And are you... are you happy with your decision? Are you able to make a commitment, work at creating a home where Dylan and I can be safe and happy? Are you able to reconcile yourself to a life without Linda? You're bound to bump into her at some point... How will you feel when you see her?'

'I don't think words can express what I might feel. Adjectives like sad, depressed, bitter, angry may not be enough. When I look into our future, I see nothing will have changed between us. We'll still be sharing the same house, each in our own world, miles apart. Can't you see the minutes and the hours drifting by? Each new year as bleak as the last?'

His words shock her. She had been sure that if Linda was out of the way they could pick up the pieces and make a go of their lives. Though, when she thinks about it, the pieces were on the floor long before Linda came on the scene. She hadn't thought much about Andrew's state of mind in the pre-Linda days. It was her own happiness that concerned her, hers and Dylan's. As long as she had her sexual needs satisfied and they had a comfortable lifestyle, nothing else mattered. She knew from the day they met they were not compatible. But he was what she was looking for; his job prospects looked good, and she liked him. Their relationship was not, and never would be, perfect, but there were compensations: Andrew enjoys his work; she likes the independence they allow each other. Now, she sees those things are not enough, that if she can't give him the missing ingredient, some other Linda will enter his life.

Chapter 34

When Linda walked out of Andrew's life, a shutter fell; it shattered her dreams, put an end to all hopes of a future with him. That was ten days ago. Since then she has gone through the motions of looking after Ben, going to her cleaning jobs, shopping, housework, putting food on the table. She had kept her sorrow hidden, thought hiding it would make it fade away and be forgotten. Each day she behaved as though nothing out of the ordinary had happened. She and Ben visited her mother on Saturday; on Sunday she took him to the park. Her smiles were empty, as fragile as windswept leaves; they belonged to no one nor to anything and, in the end, they crumbled. It was then she knew she needed help.

The following day, as soon as she finishes at Mr Roberts', Linda walks to the nearest telephone box, goes inside, looks for the Samaritans' phone number and picks up the phone. The woman at the end of the line asks how she can help; before she can reply Linda bursts into tears. For a while Linda is unable to speak; but bit by bit her sobs lessen and, finally, when she catches her breath, the words pour out. Linda tells her everything, from beginning to end. Nothing is held back. 'He's married... I had an abortion... He won't leave his wife... I have a little boy... My husband... We... I... can't go on.'

The woman gives no advice - not that Linda is looking for someone else's solution to her troubles, but when Linda steps from the telephone box she feels lighter, as though the weight of her problem has been handed to someone else. A few straggling tears roll down her cheek; she wipes them away with the back of her hand, thinking, I must pull myself together, for Ben's sake; we can't go on this way.

She faces the oncoming traffic, waits for a space and crosses the road. Each step she takes increases her resolve, pushes her forward to the resolution that is pounding her thoughts: I will, I will; I'll tell him as soon as I get in. She's frightened, doesn't know what to expect when Brian hears the words she is about to say. But it has to be now. The time is right; Brian is in the flat, Ben is in school safely out of the way. She reaches the house; her heart is beating so fast she wonders if it will survive. She opens the door, hurries up the stairs. For a brief moment she hesitates, wonders if she should wait and bide her time, if they should slip away when Brian is at work. With her mind made up, she opens the door. Holding her hands tightly together to stop them shaking, she walks into the sitting room. Brian is sat on the sofa; he doesn't take his eyes from the "Daily Mirror" when she stands in front of him. When she tells him in a voice that is loud and clear, 'Brian, I'm leaving you. I'm taking Ben with me.' He rests the paper on his lap, looks up at her and smirks. 'If you're trying to ruin my day, you'll be disappointed. I'll be glad to see the back of you. Tell you what, as you're taking the kid, I'll have the flat and all that's in it. That's only fair, isn't it?'

All the intimidating scenarios that have haunted her are blown away, as though they were nothing more than a cloud on a rainy day. He wanted her to leave as much as she wanted to go. She turns away from him, hurries out of the room and into Ben's bedroom; she scrambles through his chest of drawers, throws a few things into his gym bag. She takes a couple of shopping bags from the kitchen and goes into the bedroom, stuffs the bags with anything that might be useful. She looks at the essays she has kept hidden in her dressing table drawer. Ever since her affair with Andrew started she had neglected her writing; Andrew had been more important than attending classes. The little time they had left from their busy schedules she wanted to spend with him. She decides to let them stay, doesn't give a backward glance as she leaves the flat, gives Brian no chance to change his mind as she closes the door behind her. Her feet hardly touch the stairs; she feels as though she is flying, and it suddenly dawns on her that what she had wanted was unrealistic. Andrew couldn't escape his own marriage, so how could he rescue her. Andrew was so far out of reach she might as well have been in love with John Lennon.

She knocks on Mrs Jones' door. Mrs Jones looks from Linda to the bags overflowing with clothes. 'Linda! Are you alright?'

'Yes, I am. I'm leaving Brian. I won't be back. But I couldn't go without saying goodbye and thanking you for everything you've done for Ben and I.'

'Why... Where are you going?'

'I can't talk now. But I'll be in touch, I promise.'

It is too early to collect Ben from school, so Linda makes her way to the green space they call the park. She sits on a bench and puts the heavy bags beside her. She had expected the elation of leaving Brian to continue, but the opposite has happened; she is calm, at peace with herself. She casts her eye around the shrubs and trees that enclose the grass where she is sat. In many ways the park has been a life saver: it had provided an escape from the flat; it was a place where she could gather her thoughts; it gave Ben room to play. She remembers the summer days, the picnics, the ball games, the quiet times when she had the little oasis to herself, and she whispers a prayer of thanks.

She arrives in the playground with time to spare. Wishing the school door to open, she stands with her back to the boundary wall, away from the crowd of waiting mothers. The children start to pour out onto the playground and she scans the sea of heads to find Ben's dark curls. She waves; he spots her, runs over and looks down at the three bags next to her feet. 'What's all that stuff?' he asks.

'We're going to spend some time with Nan.' She picks up his gym bag and gives it to him.

He takes the bag asking, 'What, now? What about school?'

'Don't worry about school. I'll ring them and explain we're taking a little holiday.'

'But it's not holiday time.'

'We'll make it holiday time; just this once.'

'How long are we going for?'

'I'm not sure yet.'

'What about Dylan? I'll have to tell him, he'll wonder where I am.'

Linda looks across the playground. Pattie and Dylan are walking towards the school gate. 'Okay,' she says, 'but don't be long.'

Ben drops the gym bag and runs towards them. Pattie and Dylan stop when they hear him call. Linda's eyes remain fixed on Ben as he talks to Dylan. Pattie says something to Ben; he replies, and she turns her head towards Linda. Briefly, their eyes meet. Then Pattie takes Dylan's hand and they walk through the school gate.

Ben runs back to Linda; she picks up his bag and gives it to him. 'Come on,' she says. 'Let's go.'

'Linda! What are you doing here? Come in. Ben, let me take that bag. Give me your coats. Sit by the fire. I'll put the kettle on. Are you hungry? I'll make some sandwiches.'

Gloria rushes into the kitchen and Linda sits by the open fire with Ben on her lap. She wonders how she is going to explain the course of events to Gloria, how Ben will react to the news that they are not going back to the flat. Soon Gloria is in the room with a tray full of food and drinks. She puts the tray onto the floor next to the hearth, passes a glass of squash to Ben, then puts a steaming cup of tea on the floor next to Linda. 'Help yourselves to sandwiches,' she says as she sits next to them; she looks at Linda. 'What's happened?'

Linda shifts Ben from her lap, gives him a kiss on his cheek and says, 'I've a few things to say to Nan. I want you to take your bag upstairs and unpack. I'm sure Nan won't mind if you eat in your bedroom; choose what you want, and I'll bring it up for you. After you've eaten, find a few games we can play later.' She waits for him to fill his plate, takes it from him, then follows him up the stairs.

Leaving Ben happily propped up on the bed with a 'Beano' comic and a plate of ham sandwiches, Linda goes downstairs and walks back into the room. Closing the door behind her, she says, 'I've left him, Mum.' She sits on the sofa next to Gloria and turns to face her. 'Can we stay here? It won't be forever, just until we find a...'

'Hush; there's no need for that. You can stay as long as you like. This is your home.'

Linda knew her mother would say those words, that it would be a hurdle to cross. It isn't that she's ungrateful; it's just she doesn't want Ben growing up in the kind of environment that she'd had. Council estates have an unspoken set of rules; if you want to get on with your neighbours there are priorities you must adhere to: a clean house, a neat garden, the whitest of white on the washing line. They are a set of values you'd be stupid to ignore. As for ambitions, they are governed by the division of sex and class. Inverted snobbery is what the proletarians are proud of. One thing Andrew taught her was, 'You don't have to stay in a working-class rut, not if you don't want to,' and she wants Ben to aim high.

'Thanks, Mum. I appreciate the offer. It's good to know we don't have to be in a rush, but I don't want to live here permanently. I want to be independent. I want a place of our own. I want Ben and I to have a new start.'

'That's up to you Linda, but the offer's there. Tell me, what's happened?'

Linda takes a deep breath before saying, 'I reached a point when I knew I had to leave. I couldn't carry on living with someone I hate. The atmosphere in the flat was beginning to affect Ben. He's been very quiet. I've caught him sucking his thumb and rocking a few times; I was worried about him. When I told Brian I was leaving he told me he was glad to see the back of me, so it was what we both wanted. All those years of being scared of what might happen if I left and all I had to do was walk out.'

'You should have walked out ages ago. I've been expecting you ever since you told me what's going on in your marriage. I should have insisted you left then. What about that man, the one you told me about, Andrew? What's happening with him? You said you loved him. Is there any chance you might get together? I know he's married, but what kind of marriage is that! You know what I mean... they can't be any more happy than you were.'

'They're not, but he won't leave her, and I'm not prepared to be his mistress; it's as simple as that. Though I don't regret the times we spent together. Andrew showed me that love is possible, that there's something better than what I had. Without him I may not have...'

Linda stops speaking when the door opens and Ben walks into the room; he is carrying an empty plate and colourful box. 'Does anyone want a game of snakes and ladders?' he asks.

It's just gone eleven when Gloria goes into her bedroom. Before going into the room where she is sleeping, Linda creeps in to look at Ben. She thinks he is asleep, then he turns to look at her. 'How long are we staying?' he asks.

She sits on the edge of the bed. 'I don't know...' She looks down at her hands wondering how to reply; then, realising truth is the only answer, she says, 'We're not going back to the flat. We'll stay here until we find a place of our own.' She thought he might have questions to ask, so waits a minute. When he doesn't say anything, she says, 'It's like this... Daddy and I haven't been getting along very well. We thought it would be better if I left. It's easier for me to look after you than Daddy, so you're going to live with me.'

'What kind of place will we live in?'

'I don't know; what kind of place would you like?'

'Somewhere near Dylan but in the country.'

'We won't be able to live near Dylan. I think it's better for me and Daddy if we live a bit further apart, but maybe we can find a place in the country.'

'If I can't live near Dylan can I have a dog?'

'Perhaps; it depends where we're living.'

'I'd like a dog.'

Linda smiles. 'Okay, we'll look for a place where we can have a dog.'

It has been three weeks since Linda rang Mr Roberts and Mr Thomas to tell them she had moved away and wouldn't be able to work for them anymore. Since then she has visited the Job Centre every day, scoured the job columns in newspapers, and read countless adverts in shop windows. She is beginning to feel there's nothing for her. Gloria's constant nagging hasn't helped; she insists that Linda gets in touch with Brian because: 'Paying maintenance is the least he can do.' What Linda would like is to be financially independent and never see him again. What makes it all worthwhile is the positive change in Ben's behaviour: the thumb-sucking and rocking has stopped.

Linda is five minutes early when she enters the Job Centre. She sits down, waits for her number to be called, then goes into the allocated cubical. She is now on first name terms with the woman who is interviewing her. 'It's really difficult looking for work and a home at the same time,' Linda tells Sandra. 'What do I look for first, the job or the house? I still haven't enrolled Ben for school; how can I when I don't know where we'll be living!'

'Have you tried looking in "The Lady" magazine?' says Sandra. 'Don't be put off by the name; all sorts of people advertise in it: people who are looking for live-in staff, housekeepers, child-minders and such like, but it would give you a place to live and a salary.'

As soon as Linda arrives home, she joins Ben at the kitchen table. He is engrossed in a puzzle; undisturbed, Linda opens "The Lady" magazine and finds the jobs vacant page. The words scream out at her: "WANTED: live-in housekeeper for widower and young son. Must have experience with children and like animals. Write to Mr D. Barker, Elm House, Upton Down, Somerset, or call 84629." Gloria can be heard cleaning the upstairs rooms. Linda picks up her purse, tucks the magazine under her arm and goes into the hallway. She stands at the bottom of the stairs and calls, 'Won't be long, Mum. I'm just going down to the phone box.' before Gloria has time to reply, she grabs her coat and leaves the house.

'...My wife died three months ago,' his voice tells her. 'I work away quite a bit. I travel the West Country, Cornwall, Devon, as well as Somerset, collecting art and craft work. I'm a sort of go-between for artists and gallery owners. Peter is nine; he misses his mum terribly. I have to make sure the person living with us will be understanding and sympathetic. What about you? Tell me about yourself.'

'Well, I'm a single parent. One of the reasons I was attracted to your advertisement is because I have a son. Ben is eight; it will be good for him to have another child in the house. I love children; I would have had more if circumstances had been different. As for animals, Ben will be over the moon; he's been pestering me to get a dog. At the moment I'm living with my mother.'

'Upton Down is very quiet; not much goes on here.'

'It sounds just what we're looking for.'

I have to be careful who I employ, so I hope you don't mind me asking, do you have a husband, and if you do, where is he?'

'We're separated; if you're asking because you're worried we might get back together, I can assure you we won't. I've started divorce proceedings.'

The village of Upton Down was a short bus ride from Taunton Railway Station. When Linda steps down from the bus, she watches it move away, then looks at the drawn map that David Barker had posted to her. She moves away from the bus stop and, keeping the map in her hand, she follows David's directions. They take her past a higgledy-piggledy collection of stone-built cottages, with slate roofs and tiny front gardens. She passes an ancient-looking pub with ivy clad walls and small casement windows. She stops to look in at a post office that also sells newspapers, bread, potatoes and a mishmash of things that people might need. She carries on walking; other than a delivery van parked outside a house, and what must be the driver hammering on the door, there is little sign of life. Within minutes she arrives at the edge of the village. She looks at the map again; then looks at David Barker's house.

The house is detached, modern in design, with cement rendered walls. It's an ugly building, quite out of character with the rest of the village, incongruous against the quaint cottages and pub. She opens the metal gate and a dog immediately barks. A man's voice shouts, 'Bob! Be quiet.' The dog stops barking; the door opens and a man with red hair and a bushy beard calls, 'You must be Linda. I'm glad to see you.' Picking her way through an accumulation of balls, bats, a roller skate, a scooter and a child's bike, she makes her way along the path towards him. She reaches the door, and David gives her a broad smile. 'Come in. Excuse the mess,' he says.

She steps inside and follows him into a sitting room. A large black Labrador sniffs her hand. David moves a pile of comics from a sofa and invites her to sit down. A tortoiseshell cat jumps on her lap. 'As you can see,' he says, 'the place needs a woman's touch. My wife was ill for nearly a year before she died, and things got out of hand. I'd offer you a cup of tea but we're out of milk. I hope the place isn't putting you off.'

She shakes her head. 'No, not at all. I've cleaned places in a far worse state than this. Let me get the milk. I could do with a cup of tea.'

'Well, if you don't mind. The Post Office sells milk. I'll put the kettle on. Let me give you some money.'

'No, the milk's on me,' she says as she puts the cat down onto the floor.

She follows David out of the room. 'Take your time,' he tells her as he opens the front door. 'You might as well get to know the neighbourhood.'

Chapter 35

Pattie hasn't noticed the nights getting shorter, how much milder the days have become; her winter coat still hangs on the hook in the hallway, her summer clothes are still packed in suitcases waiting to be aired. Spring has come and gone without her giving a thought as to what season it might be.

It was just after midnight when Pattie woke. Andrew was next to her, snoring gently. The snores didn't disturb her, but she couldn't get back to sleep. Her mind had been crowded with what she should or should not do and she had lain awake for what seemed like hours. Now a crack of light is shining through the gap in the curtains, and she realises she must have fallen asleep again. Andrew is not next to her. She looks at the clock; it's nearly eleven-thirty. He and Dylan would have left the house hours ago. She moves the covers aside and gets out of bed, walks to the window, pushes back the curtains, and gazes down onto the garden. The withered remains of daffodils line the path; behind them decomposing tulips have collapsed amongst the emerging annuals. Life outside the house seems to have left her behind; it's as though a blast of cold air blew her inside out, leaving her frozen in a place she can't escape from. She goes back to the bed, sits on the crumpled sheets and picks up her book from the bedside table. She opens it, looks through the pages, tries to remember where she left off, what the story is about. She puts her legs up onto the bed. Leaving the book at her side, she rests her head against the pillow. The house has an eerie silence; without Dylan the pulse that makes it home is extinguished. Andrew's offer to take Dylan to a miniature railway event was to give her time to spend as she would like. The trouble is, when she's alone she dwells on the trap she has put both Andrew and herself in.

She thought with Linda out of the way their marriage stood a chance. That if they shared a bed, promised each other not to get sexually involved with other people, things would improve. She has tried hard to be the sort of woman she thinks Andrew would want, has done everything within her power to be faithful and agreeable. She keeps her mouth shut when her instinct tells her to argue, has been a virtue of patience when it comes to love-making. She fakes orgasms. Fakes interest in his work. To prove to Andrew she was serious when she said casual sex is a thing of the past, she cancelled her piano lesson - she didn't tell Andrew that Tony is now engaged to some girl, that he told Pattie sex between him and her had to stop.

She decided a night out, just the two of them, would put a spark into their relationship. She talked it over with Carol, who agreed to have Dylan for the night. Pattie booked a table at a smart new restaurant in town. She bought a dress with Andrew in mind, one he would approve of, a classic design but not old fashioned, a hint of cleavage but not too revealing. She made an appointment with her hairdresser, had her hair cut in the style she wore when they first met.

The evening was a waste of time and money; other than talking about Dylan, they have nothing in common, nothing to say to each other: they didn't bother with coffee. Despite her efforts, despite sharing a bed with him, they might as well be living on different planets.

They still sit together most evenings, reading or watching television, but she knows he would prefer to be elsewhere. When they make love, it isn't her he is thinking of. She has asked herself where all her endeavours are leading, certainly not to a happy marriage.

She realises she must face the truth: Andrew is only with her because he doesn't want to lose Dylan. When Dylan leaves home, so will Andrew. She wonders why she is waiting for the inevitable; she can bring this farce of a marriage to an end with just a few words: 'Go to her.'

Acknowledging that there is no blissful future with Andrew is like opening a prison door. Okay, she will have to get used to the fact that Linda is his woman, but she can hold her head up high knowing she was the one who told him to go to her. She is sure that Andrew will be generous, financially and otherwise. He will want to spend time with Dylan; he may let her keep the house. When she thinks about it, she can see how liberating being on her own will be: she can stop pretending to be someone she is not.

She stands up from the bed with her mind made up; she will tell Andrew she is not going to take Dylan to Ireland, that if he loves Linda he must go to her. But first she needs to find out where Linda is living; it will be her gift to Andrew, her way of saying sorry.

Pattie is aware that finding Linda may not be easy - Linda kept herself to herself; to her knowledge, Linda had no close friends. She tries to think of someone who might know of Linda's whereabouts. The only person that comes to mind is Brian. He is the last person she would want to speak to, but he is bound to know Linda's address.

She quickly gets dressed, is about to leave the house, when she suddenly remembers Linda's neighbour, the old lady who lives in the ground floor flat. The woman had answered the door when Pattie called to persuade Brian to go to the school play. She tries to remember the woman's name and then it comes to her, Mrs Jones. Linda had been fond of the old lady; they may have kept in touch.

Pattie stands in front of the house where Linda had lived. Hoping it will be the old lady that answers, she rings the bell. The door opens. 'Good afternoon, Mrs Jones,' says Pattie. 'You probably won't remember me. It was a while back when we last spoke. I'd called to speak to Linda and you answered the door. My son Dylan and Ben were great friends. Dylan is really missing Ben and wants to send him a letter. Linda gave me her address, but I've foolishly mislaid it. She always spoke fondly of you, so I thought to myself Mrs Jones will know where she is living. Do you know the address? Can you let me have it?'

The old lady looks at Pattie with suspicion. 'I do know, but I can't let you have it. In her letter, Linda asked me not to pass it on to anyone. I'm sorry, I must do as she asks. I'm sure she has her reasons. Her husband's still living in the flat, but... I don't know if he'll help you... I'm sorry.'

When the door closes, Pattie is left wondering what to do next, if it is worth speaking to Brian, what sort of reception she will get. She puts her finger on the bell and waivers, wondering whether to stay or go, then presses it.

She stands waiting. Other than Mrs Jones, she is beginning to think the house is deserted. Then she hears the click of the latch and the door opens. This time a big breasted woman, probably in her mid-twenties, with black back-combed hair - obviously dyed - wearing fluffy pink slippers and a scruffy red dressing gown and smoking a cigarette, stands in the doorway. She looks Pattie up and down, takes the cigarette out of her mouth, flicks the ash onto the floor and says, 'Yes?'

'Is Brian in?'

'What do you want him for?'

'I think that's my business.'

The woman takes another drag from the cigarette, then throws the butt onto the pavement. 'Well if you're not going to tell me, I might as well shut the door.'

'I'm trying to get in touch with Linda; I want to ask Brian for her address.'

'Brian's out. On Saturdays he goes to the betting shop, or he might be in a pub. I don't know where he is or when he'll be back. I wouldn't waste your time looking for him. He won't tell you. I don't mention her name; it makes him mad. He had a hard time with her, what with all the blokes she slept with. He nearly killed one of them. Take my advice, keep out of his way.'

The door closes, and Pattie breathes a sigh of relief. Brian may have had the answer she's looking for but she's glad she didn't have to face him.

Searching her mind for a face, a name of someone who might know where Linda is, she walks back to the car. She suspects that Linda is living with her mother, but without knowing her mother's name she will be impossible to find. She then thinks about Linda's employers; surely, she wouldn't have left without telling them where she is going. The chemist shop where Linda worked is a short walk away. Feeling hopeful, Pattie turns around and goes there.

Mr Thomas is emphatic. 'No, she didn't leave an address. It was all so sudden, left me in the lurch she did. She didn't ring till the following day. She said I owed her money. I argued, but she insisted. Then she told me to give the money to a charity. She's an odd one is Linda.'

After thanking him, Pattie drives to Roberts' Newsagent. 'I'm worried about her,' says Mr Roberts. 'It's not like Linda to let me down. Something must have happened for her to run off like that... Let me know if you find her.'

It's past their usual tea time when Pattie arrives home. She walks into the kitchen; Andrew and Dylan are sat at the table eating. 'There's soup on the stove; you might have to reheat it,' says Andrew. 'Have you had a good day?'

'I'll have some later,' she says as she joins them at the table. 'Yes, I've had a lovely time. I've been in the park enjoying the weather and reading my book. Tell me about your day.'

For the rest of the evening, Pattie is preoccupied. Finding Linda has grown into a mammoth task. She could tell Andrew he is free to go, and he can look for Linda himself. The trouble is, leaving it to Andrew won't have the same impact as giving him the news herself.

Another restless night brings to mind a few more potential leads. So, on Monday morning, after seeing Dylan into school, she goes to the school secretary's office and requests an urgent meeting with the Headmaster. The meeting with the Headmaster is brief. His reply is curt: Linda's address is confidential.

Pattie remembered Linda talking about the writers' group she attended, and calls into the library; the group disbanded months ago through lack of interest.

Pattie had just about given up any hope of finding Linda, was considering telling Andrew she had been looking for her and her reasons behind it, when she has a phone call from Carol. 'Guess what?' says Carol. 'I know where Linda is.'

'You do? How? When? Where is she?'

'Hang on; let me tell you. I happened to bump into Dorothy Smith; do you remember her? She has a son called Stephen. He used to hang around with Dylan and Ben in the playground sometimes. Well, she told me she saw Linda and Ben at the railway station. Of course, Stephen ran over to them, and Ben told him they were on their way to see his Nan. He also told him that they were living in Somerset, a place called Upton Down. I looked on a map. Upton Down is tiny, not much more than a hamlet; you'll have no trouble finding her.

Pattie puts the receiver down and looks at her watch. Andrew will be home in less than an hour. Carol has offered to collect Dylan from school and give him tea, which gives Pattie plenty of time to talk to Andrew undisturbed.

While Pattie waits for Andrew to arrive, she becomes as jittery as a kitten. One minute she is focused and calmly rehearsing what she is going to say, the next she is on her feet looking out of the window, anxious to see him. One moment she is wondering if she is doing the right thing, the next she can't wait to tell him the news. She is ordering herself to calm down when she hears the squeak of the garden gate. All her plans are forgotten when he steps into the house; she is waiting for him. Before he has time to speak, she says, 'I know where Linda is.'

He puts his briefcase onto the floor and gives her a quizzical look. 'What are you talking about?'

'I told you; I know where Linda is.'

'Where's Dylan?' he asks in a worried voice.

'Dylan's with Carol; he's having tea there. Come and sit down. I want to talk to you, Andrew.'

Leaving the briefcase on the floor, he follows her into the sitting room. 'What's this all about?'

'Sit down, and I'll explain.' She stands in front of him. 'It's never going to work between us, Andrew. I've been thinking about it. I can't force you to love me. I shouldn't have stopped you leaving.'

'I don't understand. You were quite clear about what you wanted and how you felt about Linda.'

’I was wrong. I realise that now. What I want to tell you is I know where she is, and that you should go to her.’

‘But... What... What about Dylan?’

‘Listen to me; I’m not going to take Dylan away. I’m sorry I ever said it. Dylan needs you; you need to be near him. We’ll work something out.’

‘I don’t know. This has all come as a shock.’

‘Andrew, what’s the use of us being together? Neither of us is happy, but you can be. That’s if you still love her. Do you?’

‘Yes.’

‘Go to her then. Tell her you want to be with her. Go before it’s too late.’

Chapter 36

Linda takes the plate of tarts from the shelf where she had left them to cool out of reach of the children and puts them onto the kitchen table. The bang of the back door being pulled open makes her look round. The boys are on the garden step kicking off their boots. Leaving the door open, they come into the kitchen. Their eyes dart towards the table, as though the smell of warm pastry and strawberry jam had sent out a signal. Ben's sun-tanned face is smiling broadly, his hair a mass of dark tangled curls, his jeans worn away at the knee from crawling in and out of the bamboo den that he and Peter have constructed in the middle of the lawn. The hours of rough and tumble play have changed Ben almost beyond recognition. He is no longer the pale-faced scrawny kid he used to be. There is a curve of muscle to his calves and arms, a certainty in his movements that says his confidence has soared.

The dog has followed the boys into the house; it sits beside Ben with its tail thumping the floor, its head held high sniffing the air. Peter wipes his hand across his forehead, leaving a smear of dirt as he says, 'I'm thirsty.'

'Me too, and hungry,' says Ben, looking at the tarts.

Suddenly the dog makes a jump towards the table. Ben grabs the dog's collar and pulls him away. 'Take him outside,' says Linda. Peter picks up a bottle of squash from the worktop and carries it to where the glasses are kept. The dog is refusing to move. Linda takes the dog's collar from Ben, then, trying to make herself heard above the boys' chatter and the dog's whine, she shouts, 'Wait a minute; wash your hands.' She drags Bob across the floor towards the door, pushes him outside, saying, 'You can come in later.'

She closes the door, stands with her back to it, engrossed in the domestic chaos that surrounds her: Ben and Peter's chatter as they wash their hands at the kitchen sink, the bowl filled with fallen apples waiting to be made into chutney, the kittens curled asleep in a basket by the radiator, is a heaven she never thought would be hers. The move to Upton Down has brought many other unexpected gifts: a love of gardening, star-filled nights, a hedgehog living under the shed, feeding a fox and her cubs at dusk, a dawn chorus to wake her. She is amazed that she can feel this content. That she doesn't seem to have a worry or a care in the world. That she can enjoy every minute of her day and want no more.

With their eyes fixed on the tarts, the boys wipe their hands on the towel. Linda picks up the squash and pours a little into each glass. She is about to take them to the tap when the doorbell rings. She puts the glasses down. 'I wonder who that is... carry on boys. No more than two each, mind.' She goes into the hallway, walks swiftly to the door, and opens it.

Seeing him doesn't make sense. It can't be, not you, not Andrew, not here, not in this house, not in Upton Down where obscenity and scandal are what you read about in the newspapers. Not in this village where the most talked about thing happened four years ago when Mrs Jenkins left her husband for the postman. Not in this life, this place she calls home. She puts her hand against the door ready to push it shut.

'Can I come in?' he asks.

His voice jolts her into realising that this is really happening, that he is standing in front of her asking to be invited into her world. She turns to look down the hallway.

The kitchen door is open; Ben and Peter are larking about. She looks back at Andrew, is ready to slam the door, changes her mind, nods her head, and steps aside to let him in.

He comes into the house and she points to the sitting room, saying, 'In there.' She goes down the hallway. 'I won't be a minute,' she tells the boys, then she closes the door and goes back to the sitting room. He is sat on the sofa. She chooses an armchair, six feet away from him with a view of the garden. She gathers together the accumulation of comics left on the seat, puts them onto the floor, and perches on the edge of the chair like a fledgling ready for flight. 'How did you know I was here?' she asks.

'Dorothy Smith's son, Stephen, spoke to Ben. You and he were at the railway station. Ben told him you were living in Upton Down. Dorothy told Carol and she told Pattie. I called into the Post Office when I got here, and they told me where to find you.'

Linda remembers the day. She had only just got off the train when she spotted Dorothy, had been looking for a way to avoid her when Stephen saw Ben and it was too late. 'What do you want? Why are you here?' she asks.

'I wanted to see you. I've been worried about you. I need to talk to you.'

She remains silent; she has nothing to say. What happened between them is a thing of the past; it has nothing to do with her life now. Memories of things that were said and done have been put into a time capsule, not forgotten, but out of reach.

She continues to watch him, her hands in her lap, all emotion stripped from her eyes, her face impassive, any feelings of love for him stored away in the back of her mind.

'It's over between me and Pattie,' he says. 'We've come to a decision; we're going to live apart. She knows I'm here. We talked it over and she's not going to take Dylan away. I won't lose him. I'm free. We can be together: you, Ben and me; the three of us.'

How she had longed to hear those words, but now is too late: the words are as dead as her aborted baby, as meaningless as her barren womb. His rejection had smashed all hope of a future with him. The respect she'd had for him smothered by Pattie's control.

'Ben and I are settled,' she says. 'We're happy. I have a job and a home; it suits us to stay.'

'I can give you a home. You won't have to work.'

'I'm not going to disrupt Ben's life; Peter, the boy I look after, is like a brother to him.'

'Children are resilient. Dylan can stay with us at weekends; they were like brothers.'

She shakes her head. 'Ben loves it here; I'm not going to take him away. David, the man I work for, Peter's father, has asked me to marry him.'

'Oh... and will you?'

'Maybe.'

'I've never stopped loving you, Linda. You knew the situation, the pressure I was under; if you were faced with the choice I had to make you would have done the same; you would have chosen Ben, I know you would have. But all that's changed; we are both free to do as we like. We can make a home together. Pattie will give me a divorce; if you want to, we can get married.'

'It's a bit late for that. I told you, Ben is settled. I won't disrupt his life again.'

'But is this what you want? What can this man give you that I can't?'

'Trust; I trust him. There's no wife hanging around, divorced or otherwise.'

'So, you will marry him?'

'When my divorce is finalised I probably will.'

'You won't even consider my proposal?'

'No.'

'Do you want me to go?'

She stands up. 'Yes, I've work to do. David will be home soon. I never told him about you, so I would like you out of the house.'

He follows her into the hallway; she opens the door. He touches her hand, looks into her eyes. 'It's goodbye then?'

Looking away from him, she says, 'Yes.'

He leaves the house. She watches him walk down the path. He reaches the gate, opens it and steps on to the pavement. Other than the gate swinging on its hinges, no one would know he had ever been there. He is wearing the pale blue jacket that suits him so well: the roughness of its material on her arm, the softness of his hair when her fingers touch the collar, seeps into her memory. Her eyes trace his shape, his every movement. He walks past the cottages, turns the corner, and disappears from sight.

~

Epilogue

~ July 2006 ~

Linda recognises Pattie straight away. She has put on weight and her once lovely strawberry blonde hair is now a kind of washed-out peachy white, but it's undeniably her. Pattie is standing behind a young couple; they seem to be having trouble explaining their destination to the bus driver. Linda uses the hold-up to sit and stare, to take in every detail. Pattie is dressed in the bright colours she always loved, though the shocking pink scarf and turquoise coat are shabby and unfashionable. Seeing Pattie waiting patiently to pay her bus fare, a Tesco carrier bag in her hand, a resigned look on her face, is so out of character with the Pattie she once knew. Linda begins to wonder why. The young couple move away, and Pattie takes their place. She picks up her ticket, turns to look down the gangway, and Linda lifts her hand.

Pattie's eye catches someone waving; she looks at the woman's face. If the woman hadn't drawn attention to herself, she would have walked straight past her. Linda's once sleek dark hair is steel grey. Cut short in a masculine style that takes away the soft feminine look that Pattie had envied. Pattie walks down the aisle; Linda's smile casts creases across a weather-worn face bare of cosmetics. She moves her bag from the seat next to her and Pattie sits down.

'Linda, my God! Fancy seeing you; the last thing I heard, you were living in the country. But that was... How many years ago...? I lose track of time. Tell me, what are you doing?'

'Pattie... I thought it was you when you got on. I don't know how many: an age ago. I'm visiting... We're staying with my husband's son; Peter and his family live here. I thought I'd take the opportunity to go into town. What about you? Are you still in the same house?'

'No, I'm in Redland. I've been there a while. In fact, I get off the next stop. There's so much to talk about. How long are you here?'

'We've only got another day.'

'You must come tomorrow then. Come to mine.' Pattie puts her hand into the carrier bag she is holding and pulls out a handbag. She opens it, searches inside until she finds a scrap of paper and a pen, then, resting the paper on the bag, she hurriedly writes her address. 'Here,' she says giving the paper to Linda. She rings the bell and stands up. 'Come about two.'

Linda watches Pattie move down the gangway; she gets off the bus and Linda looks at her through the window. Pattie mouths, 'See you tomorrow.' The bus moves away. Linda looks at the address. Pattie never mentioned Andrew; she said, I'm in Redland, not we.

Linda stands in a small front garden dominated by an overgrown laurel hedge and four overflowing dustbins. The building is a large Victorian semi, similar in style to Andrew and Pattie's previous house. She looks at the list of residents' names and presses Pattie's bell.

Pattie takes a quick look in the mirror, telling herself, I must get something done to my hair. She leaves the flat, makes her way down to the ground floor and opens the door. Now that Linda is standing in front of her, she can see who this woman is: her slender body, the way she lowers her head to compensate for her height, are unmistakable.

'Come in,' says Pattie. 'It's a bit of a climb; I'm up on the top floor.'

'That's alright,' says Linda as she steps inside. 'I'm used to it. David and I do a lot of hill walking. We've a very active German Shepherd, which is why we don't stay away too long.'

Linda is surprised by how shabby the garden and house is, and that Pattie's fluffy, backless, yellow slippers are so worn they are falling off her feet. Considering how dangerous broken slippers can be on a threadbare stair carpet, she wonders why Pattie hasn't replaced them.

'Let me take your coat,' says Pattie when they reach the top. She watches Linda undo her buttons, wonders why Linda, who was once so elegant, who could fashion herself a designer outfit from something she'd found in a jumble sale, is now wearing a gabardine raincoat and brogues. Beneath the coat is a tweed skirt and hand-knitted cardigan, an outfit that would grace the Queen, thinks Pattie as she takes the coat and drapes it over the banister. 'Come into the sitting room,' she says. 'Sit down. I'll make us a drink; tea or coffee?'

From what Linda can see of the flat, it's almost identical to the one that she and Brian had lived in: four small square rooms, similar in size and shape, sloping ceilings with hardly enough space to put a bed, let alone anything else to make your life comfortable. Listening to the clatter coming from the kitchen, Linda casts her eye around her. She wonders why Pattie's circumstances seem to be so reduced, and where is Andrew? Photographs are displayed on a sideboard. Linda gets up from her chair, walks to the sideboard and picks one up. The young man with the toddler on his back must be Dylan; the laughing woman at his side holding the hand of a young girl might be his wife. She puts the photograph down and picks up another. The same family smile out at her; Dylan is stockier than his father, but every bit as handsome. The woman under his arm is the sort of daughter-in-law any mother would love. She picks up every photograph. Andrew's image is not there. Linda hears Pattie come into the room. Almost dropping the brass frame, she spins round. 'I guess this is Dylan,' she says.

'Yes, he and his family live in Ireland; Tom is two and Ella's seven.' Pattie puts the tray onto the small coffee table and walks to where Linda is standing. She takes the photograph, gazes at it a while before saying. 'They would like me to move over and join them. I miss them terribly, but I was never one for rural, which is why I left Ireland in the first place. I visit a couple of times a year. They're very settled. They won't come back. Dylan and Kate run a holiday business letting cottages to rich Americans. They run the business between them. They do everything: cleaning, cooking, picking people up from the airport, bookkeeping. I wonder how they manage with two small children, but they both pull their weight; they work as a team. It's not like the old days when men thought it was their right to be waited on hand, foot, and finger.' She puts the photograph down and goes to the tray. 'Do you take sugar?' she asks.

'You're lucky to have grandchildren,' says Linda, taking her coffee. 'My husband's son, Peter, has two children, but Ben's not the settling down type.'

'How is Ben?' asks Pattie.

'He's well. David took him on as a partner; they supply and deliver art work to galleries. Ben's got a Fine Arts degree; he's made a bit of a name for himself as an artist, in a small way.'

'Where are you living?'

'We're still in Upton Down. I've been there thirty years. David's been there longer than that; he lived there with his first wife. She died, which is why I ended up working for him. Ben's still with us. The only time he left home was when he went to college; we'll probably have him forever. Looking after two men, a dog and a couple of cats, while trying to keep the house and garden in some kind of order, keeps me busy. When I've a minute, I like to write. I've had a few short stories accepted for publication... in women's magazines... it's just a hobby. We visit Peter every couple of months. I enjoy seeing the children but at this time of the year I'm always glad to get home. Ben will keep the house in order and feed the animals. He'll pick the runner beans and freeze them, but I can't rely on him to do any watering; it seems to go clean out of his head. You're lucky to have grandchildren. I'd like a grandchild of my own. Peter's children call me Nan. Don't get me wrong, I love them, but it's not the same. None of Ben's girlfriends last long. Dave jokes about it; he says any more grandchildren would bankrupt us.'

'Do you hear from Brian?'

'No. We haven't been in touch for years.'

'What's David like? Are you happy?'

'Yes, I've been lucky; he's a good man. I couldn't ask for better. What about you? Is Andrew... I guess you're not together.'

'I'm on my own. I never got over the break-up of my marriage, which is why I couldn't live with anyone again. When you left, we did try to make it work, but in the end we decided to separate... It was all really hard... It was me that told Andrew to go and talk to you; he had agonised about going. When he came back, he was deeply depressed... Why didn't you go with him?

Linda is startled by the question; it was said so abruptly she feels disconnected, set adrift between the woman she had once been and the woman she is now. It opens an even bigger question: is her life a sham? Does she play her part so well she doesn't know who she is, whether she is happy or not? 'I... I couldn't...,' she stammers. 'It was too late; I had Ben to think of. I didn't want to disrupt him, not again. Andrew said he couldn't love Ben, that Ben could never take Dylan's place; it wouldn't have worked between us. I couldn't live with someone who didn't love my child.'

'Andrew wasn't capable of loving anyone. Not your child nor ours, not me nor you. It was your love he wanted; he needed someone to tell him how wonderful he was.' Pattie waits for Linda to digest her words; she wants the implication of them to penetrate so deep they won't be forgotten. She watches Linda's face: no movement, no sign to tell her what is happening behind that composure. 'He took early retirement,' she says. 'He moved to Derbyshire, bought a cottage in a small hamlet miles from anywhere. I never saw him again. Dylan visited him occasionally; he never stayed long. He said Andrew looked and lived like a tramp, that the house stank of nicotine, that Andrew was a bordering alcoholic.'

'Doesn't he see him anymore?' Linda's voice is so soft Pattie lowers hers when she says, 'No, Andrew died five years ago.'

A shock goes through Linda; she had always thought she would know when death took him. A silence falls between them. There was nothing left to say. 'I think I should go,' says Linda. They both stand up, and Linda follows Pattie out of the room. Pattie hands Linda her coat and she leads her down the stairs; Pattie opens the door and it closes between them.

Pattie climbs the stairs, thinking about what she had said to Linda, wondering why she had told Linda that Andrew hadn't been able to love his own child: it wasn't true; it was Andrew's love for Dylan that prevented him leaving in the first place. It was after Linda's refusal that Andrew distanced himself from both Dylan and herself. She reaches the top of the house and goes into the flat. Why didn't she tell Linda about George, she asks herself; perhaps it was because she wanted Linda to see her as an independent woman, happy to be on her own. Which is what she is, but you don't have to be owned by a man to have a fulfilling sex life. Seeing George a couple of nights a week, going to the cinema, the occasional meal out followed by an hour or so in bed, suits her nicely. She walks into her bedroom and opens the dressing table drawer, takes out the album that holds her wedding photographs. She sits on the bed, remembering how proud she had been to have the good-looking Englishman at her side.

Still in a state of shock, Linda stands on the pavement. Pattie's words, 'Andrew died,' are ringing in her ears. She wonders what on earth she has been thinking of these past years thirty years, why she had anchored herself to the first safe harbour, refusing to acknowledge the fact that she was grieving for a lost love. And why has she spent those years regretting a decision with no foundation to say where it would have led? She always thought she would know when he had died, that the thread she had conjured would pull and... and what, she thinks... that she would be free? Five years he has been dead, and life has carried on in exactly the same way.

She thinks about David; he will probably be doing some useful little job in the garden, or around Peter's house. Soon he will start to wonder what time she'll get back, will be interested to hear how her afternoon with an old friend went. Peter and his wife will begin to prepare something special for this evening's farewell meal. In the morning, she will hug Peter's children and tell them the horse-riding lessons she had promised for when they come to stay have been arranged. At the last minute, Ben will pull out the vacuum cleaner and give the house a clean, ready for their arrival. The dog will sense they are on their way home and give a thump of his tail.

Printed in Poland
by Amazon Fulfillment
Poland Sp. z o.o., Wrocław